MUD CITY MURDERS

When four dangerous convicts escape from prison, US Marshal Ellis Stack is sent to track them down. His journey takes him through two remote mining towns. At the first, another US marshal and five deputies are murdered by the outlaws. From there, the trail leads to Mud City, where some miners have been murdered and the escaped prisoners are the main suspects. But Ellis, with the help of an Indian called Apache Joe, discovers that the blame has been laid at the wrong door . . .

FRANK FIELDS

MUD CITY MURDERS

Complete and Unabridged

LINFORD
Leicester

First published in Great Britain in 2001 by
Robert Hale Limited
London

First Linford Edition
published 2003
by arrangement with
Robert Hale Limited
London

British Library CIP Data

Fields, Frank
  Mud city murders.—Large print ed.—
Linford western library
  1. Western stories
  2. Large type books
  I. Title
  823.9′14 [F]

  ISBN 1–8439–5027–8

Published by
F. A. Thorpe (Publishing)
Anstey, Leicestershire

Set by Words & Graphics Ltd.
Anstey, Leicestershire
Printed and bound in Great Britain by
T. J. International Ltd., Padstow, Cornwall

This book is printed on acid-free paper

1

'They broke out of prison at Winnemucca three days ago, killing one guard and seriously injuring two more. The last we heard they were headed this way. Any one of them on his own means big trouble, but all four of them could lead to problems on a scale never before seen in this state.'

These words were addressed to United States Marshal Ellis Stack, who had been summoned to what had been termed a 'crisis meeting' at the governor's office. Ellis studied the pictures of four men for some time before setting them to one side, and sighing deeply.

'Just my luck,' he said. 'I had been hoping to take a few days off with my family. It seems to me that every time I make any arrangements on that score something has to happen to stop it.'

'Sure, I know just how you feel, Ellis,' replied the governor. 'I was due to take a trip back East on official business. I had intended to take my wife and son with me to give them some sort of break. My wife was really looking forward to meeting some of the other governors' wives. Now this has happened I've had to call it off. As long as those men are at large in my state, I can't be seen to be running away. That is just what certain people would accuse me of doing, but that's politics I suppose. It's something which goes with the territory, so to speak. I can't allow such a thing to happen, especially since one of those men is one Mitchel Saunders who has promised to kill me. I was responsible for sending him to prison when I was a judge.'

'He can't blame you for that, surely?' said Ellis. 'As a judge you had to act on the evidence.'

'Try telling him that,' grunted the governor. 'As far as he is concerned it was me who gave him a life sentence.

He had also threatened to kill the sheriff who arrested him and the prosecuting lawyer. Sheriff Ward has since died and the lawyer went to work back East a couple of years ago. I'm sorry, Ellis, but you'll just have to explain to your wife what has happened. I'm sure she'll understand.'

'Oh, she'll understand all right,' agreed Ellis. 'Sometimes I think her problem is that she's too understanding. It wouldn't be so bad if this was the first time, but it isn't. In fact I've lost count of how many times it has happened.'

'That's the nature of the job, I'm afraid,' said the governor. 'Mine too, even if most folk think that I do nothing all day.'

'Sure, I know that,' said Ellis. 'Knowing it doesn't make it any easier though. I've thought seriously about giving up the job more than once, but Helen won't hear of it. She's also well aware that one day I'm liable to end up on the wrong end of a bullet. For most wives that would be reason enough to want their man to quit a job like this, but not her. I guess she knows I wouldn't be happy doin' anything else.'

'She's a good woman,' agreed the governor. 'I know she is your second wife and that your son is from your first marriage, but I know she looks upon the boy as her own. Just remember though, it is just another job. Your wife and son must come first.'

'That's the problem,' grunted Ellis. 'It isn't just another job as far as I'm concerned. It's my life.'

'I know how you feel,' said the governor. 'Make me a promise, Ellis, don't go putting yourself in any unnecessary danger.'

'I never do,' assured Ellis. 'OK, I'll explain to her. Now, what do we know about these men? I remember something about Mitchel Saunders but he was a loner then. What about the other three? Did they know each other before they were in prison? Probably not, but prison can throw up some strange alliances, I

4

know; remember I speak from experience. Are they likely to stay together or split up once they are well away?'

'So many questions, Ellis,' said the governor with a slight laugh. 'Unfortunately I do not have any answers.'

'I didn't expect any,' said Ellis. 'I was just thinking aloud.'

The governor picked up the pictures and looked at the names written on the back. He then took four folders and married each picture to each folder.

'It's all here,' he said. 'The best thing you can do is take these and read all about them. The only one I know anything at all about is Mitchel Saunders and I only know about him because of the trial. I don't know a thing about him apart from that. I don't even know where he comes from.'

'What about other marshals and the army?' asked Ellis. 'Have they been informed or am I expected to do it all by myself? It wouldn't be the first time I've been promised help and it never materialized.'

'Marshal Thomas Burns and some deputies are on to it from the Winnemucca end,' said the governor. 'As for the army, they have been informed but, as ever, they claim it's a civil matter and that they cannot be expected to go out searching for outlaws. I can see their point and wouldn't have expected anything else. However, I do have a certain amount of influence and General Ives has promised to do what he can. Don't rely on help from that quarter though.'

'OK,' said Ellis, 'So it's up to me and Tom Burns. I have met him a couple of times and he seems to be a good man. What's the latest from him?'

'We had a wire from Rochester this morning confirming that they are headed this way,' said the governor. 'They were apparently making for the Carson Sink, although I doubt if they'll attempt to cross it. Burns seems to think they'll go round the edge of the Sink and on towards the Stillwater Mountains. The thing is there's an awful lot of open territory between the Carson Sink and here. A whole army could lose itself up there and never be found. That apart, we know nothing.' He looked seriously at Ellis for a moment. 'Look, Ellis, I'd be the last person to tell you how to do your job and I know you like to work alone, but do you not think that on this occasion it would be better and certainly safer if you had some deputies?'

'No, sir, I do not,' Ellis replied very firmly. 'As you say, I prefer to work alone; that way I only have myself to worry about. Secondly, if I were one of those men, I would be expecting something like a posse or even the army. With luck they won't be looking for a lone man. If I had half a dozen deputies I'd never get within a mile of them. Don't worry, if I find I can't handle it I'll soon shout. Now, if you don't mind, I'll get back to my office. I have a lot of reading and a lot of planning to do. As for a whole army getting lost out there, I think we can safely say that these men do not intend to get lost anywhere. What would be the point? We don't have to go looking for them. I suppose we could simply wait for them here since it is apparently you Saunders is out to get.'

'I would feel a lot happier if they were apprehended long before they reached me,' said the governor. 'Unlike you, Ellis, I am a devout coward.'

'I don't think so, sir,' said Ellis. 'Cowards don't become state governors.'

Ellis returned to his office and gave an order that he was not to be disturbed even if the end of the world came about. Armed with a large mug of coffee he started to read about the escaped prisoners.

The first was Mitchel Saunders, better known simply as Mitch. Age and place of birth somewhat uncertain but believed to be about thirty years old and from somewhere in Wyoming. Before being sentenced to a life term for robbing a train during which the engineer and a guard died, he had been something of a small time criminal, content to rob stores and the occasional isolated bank. However, some time before attempting to rob the train and whilst serving a two year sentence, he had led an uprising at the prison and had acquired something of a hero status. The uprising had been squashed but not without loss of life on both sides. For his part in it, Mitch Saunders had been given an extended sentence of six months, which really meant very little.

The second folder contained details of a man also convicted for robbing a train during which the guard had been killed. Michael Swann, commonly known as Lefty Swann because he was left handed. He had also been arrested on previous occasions for suspected murder, although nothing was ever proved. Aged twenty-six, born in Idaho and usually worked alone but had been known to work with other outlaws on occasions.

The third man was James Coburn,

aged twenty-four, serving twenty years for robbery and several rapes. He too had been suspected of at least two murders but again, nothing could be proved. He claimed to have been born in England but had, with his parents, emigrated to America when he was a baby.

The fourth man was Seamus Docherty, aged thirty-two, the son of Irish immigrant parents, born in New York from where he had fled to escape justice in that state. He had been convicted of several robberies of small-town stores and of robbing travellers. It seemed that his escape from prison was something of a mystery since he had less than two years of a ten-year sentence remaining. However, there was a note on his file which stated that he was suspected of being mentally unstable. He had been known to fly off in sudden uncontrollable rages and had almost beaten a fellow inmate to death in prison in an argument over a piece of dry bread. He was considered to be very dangerous.

Ellis read the files several times to make certain that he knew all there was to know. He also studied a large map and planned his next move. Eventually he went home and explained the situation to his wife. As expected, she was, outwardly at least, full of understanding.

The following morning he loaded his horse aboard the northbound train and settled himself in the first-class compartment for the long journey. There were four other first-class passengers, two of whom were obviously rather put out at having what they considered a common cowhand riding with them. Even when they discovered that he was a US marshal they did not appear too happy. Ellis had to admit that his dress was not that normally associated with first-class travellers.

The journey to the remote mining town of Eureka took just over twenty-four hours. There were three stops on the way, during which both passengers who had objected to his presence left the train and one joined. Eureka was the nearest the railroad went to the area where Ellis had planned to tackle the escaped prisoners. From Eureka onwards it was all on horseback.

The train eventually arrived in Eureka at ten o'clock the following morning and was an hour late, which was not unusual. Ellis's first call was to the telegraph office where he sent a wire notifying his arrival. Some time later a message was received from the governor's office confirming that the escaped prisoners had indeed headed for the Stillwater Mountains. It was also believed that they had been joined by three other men, although their identities were unknown. From that point onwards it was most unlikely there would be any other news from Marshal Tom Burns even if they did discover the identities of the three new men.

He made his presence known to the sheriff of Eureka, Glen Roberts, who in turn lost no time in spreading the word that a US marshal was in town.

'The miners ain't a bad bunch,' he explained to Ellis, 'but they do try to take the law into their own hands, especially when it comes to claim jumpin'. Only last week they strung a man up for stealin' gold off somebody else's claim. When that happens they clam up an' I can never find out who actually killed anyone. It ain't even that often I hear about their so-called courts either. It won't hurt for them to think a US marshal is here to see what's goin' on.'

'They'll soon find out,' said Ellis. 'I won't be here that long. I'm on my way to try and find some prisoners who escaped from Winnemucca.'

'Sure, I heard about that,' said the sheriff. 'I didn't know they were headed this way though.'

'We don't really know where they're heading for,' said Ellis. 'All we know is that they escaped from Winnemucca, went through Rochester where they picked up three more outlaws and then on to the Carson Sink and towards the

13

Stillwater Mountains. I suppose they could turn off and head almost anywhere, but there is certain information which indicates they are heading this way.'

'There's an awful lot of mountains between the Carson Sink an' here,' said the sheriff. 'Apart from the Stillwater Mountains there's the Shoshone Mountains, the Toiyabe Mountains an' then the Big Smokey Valley. I hear tell there's an awful lot of that which no white man has ever set foot on. Mind, no man in his right mind would want to go up there.'

'Do you know the mountains?' asked Ellis. 'I was hoping to find someone who does. I'm goin' to need all the help I can get.'

'No, sir,' replied the sheriff. 'Nearest I've been is the Big Smokey Valley a couple of years ago. The man you want is a trapper and hunter, name of Ben Stevens. He's an old man now an' don't go huntin' no more, but he knows them mountains better'n any man livin'.'

'Are there any other towns up there?' asked Ellis. 'I know I haven't heard of any but these days towns spring up seemingly overnight sometimes.'

'Minin' towns you mean,' said the sheriff. 'Yes, I hear tell there are a couple but I've no idea where they are. Like you say, somebody hits gold an' a town suddenly appears. When the gold runs out it disappears just as fast. I'll ask about among the miners; they get to hear if anybody finds so much as a single ounce of gold. Lord knows how, but they do. They might be a rough an' ready bunch but apart from takin' the law into their own hands when it comes to claim jumpin', they're a pretty law-abidin' lot.'

'I'd be grateful if you can,' said Ellis. 'In the meantime where can I find this Ben Stevens?'

'You won't get much sense out of him until noon when he'll be in the saloon,' said the sheriff. 'Then the best thing you can do is to go to the saloon

15

and loosen his tongue with a couple of whiskies.'

News of Ellis's arrival had certainly spread very quickly. Most of the traders were openly pleased to see him, along with most of the women in the town. The miners appeared rather more cautious and apart from a few brief acknowledgements, generally avoided him. At noon precisely, Ellis entered the saloon which proved to be empty apart from the bartender and a lone, scruffy figure slouched in a corner lovingly caressing a glass of beer. Ellis needed no telling that this was Ben Stevens. He took a bottle of whiskey and two glasses over to the table.

'Mind if I join you?' he said, setting the bottle and the glasses on the table.

'Free country, so they tell me,' muttered Stevens, hardly able to keep his eyes off the bottle. 'Two glasses. You expectin' company?'

'Nope,' said Ellis. 'I thought you might like to join me, Mr Stevens.'

'Very neighbourly of you,' said

Stevens. 'You know my name, that ought to mean somethin' but I can't think what. I long since learned that a man don't invite a complete stranger to join him in a drink unless he wants somethin'. What can I do for you, Marshal?' He glanced at Ellis's badge of office. 'Sure, I heard there was a US marshal in town. Not before time either, we could do with some proper law round here.'

'You do have a sheriff,' Ellis pointed out.

'An' about as much use as cold dishwater,' grunted Stevens.

Ellis poured out two good measures of whiskey and pushed one of them towards Stevens. After a brief, suspicious look, the glass was eagerly seized and the contents knocked back in one gulp. Ellis smiled and refilled the glass.

'I hear you're the man to ask about the mountains,' said Ellis.

'Mountains is mountains,' muttered Stevens, this time sipping at the whiskey. 'Some is bigger'n others, some is wider an' some is longer, that's all. They're all made of rock.'

'I guess so,' agreed Ellis. 'The thing is, I need to know about certain specific mountains. I need to go up towards the Toiyabe and the Shoshone Mountains.'

'No man in his right mind *needs* to go up there,' muttered Stevens. 'I hear that you used to,' said Ellis.

'An' that ought to tell you somethin', Marshal,' responded Stevens. 'Look at me. Sure, I spent most of my life up there, an' for what? All I've got to show for it is a tumbledown shack an' no money. What's so hell-fire important about a US marshal goin' up there?'

'I'm looking for some prisoners who escaped from prison in Winnemucca,' said Ellis. 'My information is that they are heading this way across the Shoshone and Toiyabe.'

'Then the best thing you can do is sit an' wait for 'em,' muttered Stevens, draining his glass. 'Yes, sir, get yourself a bottle of whiskey an' maybe a woman an wait for 'em. That's what I'd do. Let them do all the hard work.' He pushed his empty glass towards Ellis and waited expectantly. 'They won't want to stay up there too long. There's nothin' up there for outlaws unless they want to get lost for a while.'

'That's what I had planned to do,' said Ellis, refilling the glass. 'What I need to know from you is the most likely place they will appear.'

'Do they know the mountains?' asked Stevens. 'I don't think so,' said Ellis.

'Then most likely they'll follow the easy route,' said Stevens. 'That'll eventually bring 'em out at the top end of Big Smokey Valley. The only other way is if they head slightly north through the Reese Pass an' then cross the Reese River. Even then they'll have to follow the river south towards the Big Smokey Valley.'

'So it seems this Big Smokey Valley is the best place,' said Ellis.

'Only trouble with that is the size of the valley,' said Stevens. 'They call it a valley but it's a mighty wide one an' most folk don't even know they're in it. There's more'n twenty miles of flat ground so you could miss a man very easy.'

'That big,' said Ellis. 'The sheriff wasn't sure if there are any towns between the Carson Sink and here. Do you know of any?'

'I hear tell there's a couple,' said Stevens. 'There used to be a place called Jackson a few years ago between the Shoshone an' Toiyabe, but that was one of them towns what grew up overnight an' disappeared just as fast. I think a few folk stayed but I don't know for sure. Best folk to tell you about things like that is the miners. Some of them can smell gold from five hundred miles away.'

'Have you any idea how long it will take them to reach this Big Smokey Valley?' asked Ellis.

'Well now,' said Stevens, draining his glass and once again pushing it towards the bottle. 'That all depends on how fast they travel. If they is in a hurry I reckon at least six days from Winne-mucca?'

'And if they take it easy?' prompted Ellis, refilling the glass. 'No more'n ten days,' replied Stevens.

'And how long for me to get to Big Smokey Valley?'

'Two days if you don't hang about,' replied Stevens. 'Three if you take it steady. Then, like I said, you have to find 'em once you're there an' that could take for ever.'

'I haven't got that long,' said Ellis. 'Is there anywhere more likely than other places where they might show?'

'Now if it was me who was lookin' for someone, I'd head for a lone, large hill more or less in the middle of the valley. They call it Indian Smoke Hill on account of that's where the Indians used to keep a look-out an' send smoke signals.'

'So, if they left the Carson Sink four days ago and it takes me three days, that means we could arrive there at about the same time.' said Ellis. 'Mind, it is now four days ago they broke out of prison and if they take it steady it means I probably have a couple of days on them.'

'I'll take your word for it,' said Stevens. 'I ain't never had no book-learnin' so things like workin' out figures don't mean much to me.'

'Thank you for your help,' said Ellis. 'I don't think there's anything else I need to know. Keep the bottle.'

'Mighty neighbourly,' said Stevens, taking the bottle and pouring himself another drink. 'Just one thing, Marshal. Make sure you've got some warm clothes an' a good blanket. It gets mighty cold out there. I'd make sure you've got plenty of water too. Water can be mighty scarce, 'specially at this time of year. There is a few waterholes an' there's a river close by Indian Smoke Hill.'

'Warm clothes and blanket are things I always carry,' assured Ellis. 'Thanks for the advice though. Now I'll go and see if Sheriff Roberts has discovered where these towns might be.'

The sheriff had, as promised, made enquiries and had learned of two towns, both of which had appeared during the past twelve months.

'The nearest is probably nothin' more'n a whole bunch of tents,' said the sheriff. 'They tell me it's been given the name of Mud City. Apparently there's so much mud about a man can hardly move. It's between the Shoshone and Toiyabe Mountains, almost at the foot of the Shoshone, they tell me.'

'Isn't that where a town called Jackson used to be?'

'So I hear,' said the sheriff. 'I hear tell there's still a few folk out at Jackson but no more'n about a dozen so it don't really count as a town. Jackson is about thirty miles south of the Mud City. They reckon there's about three hundred miners out there.'

'And the second town?' prompted Ellis.

'Reese Pass, close to the Reese River,' said the sheriff. 'Accordin' to the miners I spoke to that's more like somethin' of a town. They tell me a few traders have moved in an' there's even a cathouse. Dependin' on who you ask, there's about two thousand folk there now.'

'Reese Pass,' mused Ellis. 'That's north of the Big Smokey Valley, isn't it?'

'I reckon you know more'n I do,' said the sheriff. 'Sure, that's it. I ain't never been up there nor do I want to. It seems somebody struck a big vein of gold just over a year ago an' it's still goin' strong. Mostly these places last about six months.'

'Mud City or Reese Pass,' mused Ellis, 'which one? Do you have a map showing the Shoshone and Big Smokey Valley?'

'Got one here somewhere,' said the sheriff, rummaging in a cabinet. 'It's a few years old but I guess things like mountains an' rivers don't change that much.'

He spread the map on the desk and pointed to where he thought Mud City would be and then at the Reese Pass. Ellis traced a finger between the two and sighed.

'I reckon there must be a hundred miles between them,' he said. 'If I choose the wrong one I might never catch them.' He found a hill more or less in the middle of the northern end of Big Smokey Valley. 'Is that what they call Indian Smoke Hill?' he asked.

'I wouldn't know,' admitted the sheriff. 'I've heard the name before but that's about all. You've got your work cut out, Marshal. What are you goin' to do?'

'I wish I knew,' sighed Ellis. 'I just wish I knew. I'll have to sleep on it.'

2

Ellis slept very well that night. The long train journey had been tiring. As he lay in his bed at the aptly named Eureka Hotel, he had started to ponder about his next move but had dropped off to sleep very quickly.

After checking with the telegraph office that there had been no messages for him, Ellis loaded his horse with a few necessary supplies, took his leave of Sheriff Glen Roberts and started on the long journey to Big Smokey Valley and Indian Smoke Hill. The only definite decision he had made was to reach the hill and then reconsider.

He eventually reached the Big Smokey Valley at about midday of the third day. It took him until almost sunset to reach Indian Smoke Hill even though it could be plainly identified from a good distance away and appeared closer than it actually was.

The hill proved to be quite a lot higher than he had anticipated, almost circular, and ascent looked most difficult. The side of the hill was almost completely made up of sheer cliffs varying from about fifty feet high and more. There appeared to be only three places where ascent would be relatively easy. He made no attempt to climb it that night.

He made camp alongside a small river and cooked himself his usual fare of dried beef and beans. He certainly was not the best cook in the world but at least the food was filling and quite welcome. As predicted by Ben Stevens, the night was very cold and he kept a fire burning.

The next morning he made his way to the top of the hill, which proved rather more difficult than he had expected and taking his horse was quite out of the question. Once at the top he had a clear view in all directions and, using a spyglass he always carried, he sat himself on a rock beneath one of the few thorntrees and scanned the distant mountains and the brush-strewn valley floor.

After about four hours he started to wonder if he was doing the right thing. In that time the only signs of life he had seen were two eagles, a few buzzards, several smaller birds, a rattlesnake coiled up no more than twenty yards away — which he ignored — several small lizards and, rather surprisingly as far as he was concerned, a solitary deer down in the valley.

After considering what to do next, he decided to sit that day out and keep watch, although he did not really expect to see anyone, particularly the outlaws.

The following morning he once again climbed the hill and scanned the distant approaches for an hour. He had already made up his mind that he was going to head across the valley in the general direction from which he expected the outlaws to approach, but he thought that one last look would be a good idea.

It was just as he was about to fold up his spyglass and make his way down the hill that a sudden, slight movement amongst the brush in the valley caught his attention. Thinking that it was probably nothing more than a deer, he raised the spyglass just to make sure.

'That ain't no deer,' he said to himself. 'It looks more like a horse.'

He studied the movements for some time and worked out that whatever or whoever it was, was about two miles away. As the object came closer he was able to make out that it was definitely a man on a horse.

'Well it ain't them, that's for sure,' he said to himself again. 'Still, I reckon I'd better check him out, he might know somethin'.'

He decided to wait until the man reached the hill rather than ride out to meet him. He kept the man in view until he was no more than 400 yards away and then he scrambled down.

As the man approached, there was

something about him which told Ellis that this was no normal traveller and, from his unkempt appearance and lack of tools, he was most certainly not a miner. He took no chances and had his gun in hand. At that point he was at the top of a small scree and about to descend.

'Hold it there, mister,' ordered Ellis, as he slid down the scree. Suddenly his descent proved quicker than he had expected as he missed his footing and fell the remaining ten feet or so.

Ellis did not see exactly what happened but he did see the horse suddenly galloping away. He had just picked himself up when, about thirty yards away, the fleeing horse suddenly collapsed as it tried to avoid a large rock and threw its rider. Ellis raced after it. The horse struggled to its feet and moved a few yards further on. The man on the ground did not move at all.

Ellis bent down to examine the man, who appeared to be alive. He was obviously unconscious and blood oozed from a cut on his head. He decided that he could not leave the man out in the now baking sun and dragged him back to the shade where he had made camp. Taking the man's gun just in case he should recover, Ellis then retrieved the horse which appeared none the worse for the fall. He bathed and cleaned the wound, splashed some water in the man's face and waited. After about ten minutes the man's eyes flickered.

'Take it easy,' said Ellis. 'You had a bad fall, that's all.'

'Thanks to you,' grimaced the man, struggling to sit up. Ellis eased him upwards. 'What the hell did you want to jump out at a man like that for?' he grunted. 'You were the last thing I was expectin'.'

'I didn't jump, I fell,' said Ellis. 'Maybe I should've made myself more obvious. I just wanted to talk to you, ask you a few questions.'

'You have a mighty funny way of talkin',' grated the man. 'What the hell did you expect me to do? All I could see was that you had a gun an' you ought to know that out here that means trouble.'

'Sorry about that,' apologized Ellis. 'I'm US Marshal Ellis Stack — '

'Marshal!' exclaimed the man.

The sudden fear in his eyes told Ellis that this man probably had good reason to fear the law. He was not too surprised since most drifters were probably wanted by the law somewhere for something.

'Yes, a marshal,' said Ellis, indicating his badge of office. 'Now from your reaction I'd say that apart from not expecting to see anyone, I am probably the last person you'd want to meet and I'm curious. Why is that? Who are you?'

'Just an honest traveller,' said the man with a slight gulp. 'There ain't no law which says a man can't travel if he wants to an' for any reason he chooses. They tell me this is a free country.'

'No, there isn't,' agreed Ellis. 'If that's all you are then you have nothing to fear.' He decided to pressure the man into saying who he was. 'I'm out here looking for outlaws,' he continued. 'Yes, sir, that's what marshals do and I think I've just found me one. I think if I take you to Eureka we will find a wanted poster out on you. You'd better tell me just who you are.'

The man was plainly very ill at ease and wiped his sleeve across his mouth. 'Got some water?' he croaked. Ellis held up his canteen but kept it out of reach and waited. 'OK, OK,' croaked the man. 'The name's Joe Daniels and I admit there is a reward out on me but it ain't much. Last I heard it was one hundred dollars.'

'That still makes you an outlaw,' said Ellis, giving him the water. 'As a man of the law it is my duty to arrest all outlaws.'

Daniels suddenly laughed and fell back on to the ground. 'I get it now,' he said. 'There's only one reason a US marshal would be out in this good-forsaken wilderness. You're out to get Mitch Saunders an' the other men who escaped from Winnemucca.'

'How do you know about them?' asked Ellis.

'I was with 'em until three days ago,' said Daniels. 'I took up with 'em in Rochester just after they'd broken out of Winnemucca. I knew Saunders from when I was in prison with him before an' he led an uprisin'.'

Although Ellis was quite certain that Daniels was not in fact one of the escaped prisoners, he pulled out the pictures he had of them and compared them to him. He was definitely not one of the escaped prisoners. He showed the pictures to Daniels, making certain that he could not read the names.

'Recognize them?' he asked.

'Sure, that one's Saunders . . . ' he indicated the correct picture. 'That's Coburn, that's Swann an' that's the madman, Seamus Docherty. The only difference is that Docherty now has a big scar on his right cheek. He apparently picked it up in a prison fight over nothin' more'n a drink of water.

I'm surprised that that's the only scar he has. At least it's the only one I saw. That man should be locked away permanently. He's completely crazy.'

'Very good,' said Ellis. 'A scar on his right cheek?' He took a pencil and drew a line on the picture. 'Like this?'

'A bit longer, closer to his mouth,' said Daniels. Ellis extended the line. 'That's it. Maybe a bit more ragged, but it'll do.'

'You are being very co-operative,' said Ellis. 'What are you wanted for?'

'That's for you to find out, Marshal,' said Daniels, with a broad grin. 'The way I figure it is that you ain't really interested in small time outlaws like me. You've been sent to help Marshal Burns get Saunders, Swann, Coburn an' Docherty. You don't have the time to take me to this Eureka place, wherever it is. I figure that if I tell you what you want to know you'll let me go.'

'You're right about me being sent to get Saunders and the others,' admitted

Ellis. 'As a US marshal it is still my duty to arrest any outlaws I come across and I might still do that. What are you wanted for?'

'I robbed a couple of stores,' said Daniels. 'Hardly what you'd call bein' a big-time outlaw.'

'Small time, big time,' said Ellis. 'It's all the same to me. Why did you split up from the others?'

'Seamus Docherty,' said Daniels. 'I don't know just how much you know about him, but he's completely mad. We came on this isolated farm an' Docherty raped an' murdered the woman just for the hell of it. I'm pretty broad minded, Marshal, but the things he made that woman do before he killed her would make any normal man sick. I might be wanted by the law but there are certain things even a man like me can't stomach an' Docherty's lust for killin' an' degradin' women is one of them. You can believe me or not, as you choose, Marshal, but I ain't never raped a woman nor murdered anyone.'

'What happened to the other people at the farm?' asked Ellis.

'There was only the woman's husband and, like most men I would guess, he tried to defend his wife. Docherty shot him too but he wasn't dead when we left. I don't think he would've lasted long though, he was hurt pretty bad. Docherty seemed to find that funny.'

There was something about the man's story which Ellis found quite believable and he was inclined to accept it.

'OK, supposing I buy that,' he said, 'there is just one thing which bothers me. If this Docherty is as bad as you say he is, why did he just let you ride away? I would have thought he might have killed you as well, or at least threatened to. Why did he and what did Saunders think about what happened?'

'Him an' Docherty had one hell of a row,' said Daniels. 'All Docherty did was laugh at him an' tell him that he needed somebody like him, somebody who wasn't afraid to kill anyone. I guess he must've been right too since all Saunders did was to tell him he couldn't go round killin' everyone they came across. Docherty told him that he'd kill anyone he'd a mind to, includin' the rest of us.'

'But he still allowed you to simply ride away,' said Ellis.

'I wasn't takin' no chances. I left in the middle of the night,' said Daniels. 'I rode as fast as I could hopin' that they wouldn't follow.'

'And the others?' asked Ellis.

'They didn't seem to care one way or the other,' said Daniels. 'I know the two who took up with Saunders along with me in Rochester were shit-scared of him but they weren't prepared to admit that they'd made a mistake. Before I left they had been talkin' about dealin' with Marshal Burns an' about robbin' some miners at a place called Reese Pass. Saunders reckoned there was enough gold there to set them all up for life.'

'What plans did they have for

Marshal Burns?' prompted Ellis.

'They planned to ambush him before they reached Reese Pass,' said Daniels. 'Don't ask me where this Reese Pass is, I ain't never been in this territory before.'

'I know where it is,' said Ellis. 'Did they know Burns has six deputies with him and they are all very experienced in dealing with outlaws?'

'Yes, they knew. It seems that Saunders knows the area pretty well,' said Daniels. 'He reckoned there was a place where Burns an' his deputies would be easy to take out.'

'And then rob the miners of their gold,' said Ellis. 'There's about three thousand of them in Reese Pass. They can't be serious about robbing them?'

'Saunders an' Docherty were deadly serious,' said Daniels. 'I got out as fast as I could that night so that's all I know. I wasn't prepared to take the risk of Docherty losin' his head an' killin' me no matter how much gold there is.'

Ellis considered the position for some

time. Under normal circumstances he would have had little hesitation in arresting Daniels and taking him back to Eureka, but it now seemed that the situation was anything but normal.

'How did they get hold of guns?' asked Ellis.

'I think they took three rifles off the prison guards,' said Daniels. 'Then I heard that they held up a gun store in Rochester. I reckon they must've done, they sure seemed to have plenty of bullets an' some real fancy-lookin' guns which looked new.'

'OK, Daniels,' Ellis eventually said. 'It's your lucky day. I'm letting you go. As you say, I have far more important outlaws to deal with right now. Just remember this though. If, when all this is over, I find you within five hundred miles of any town in this state, I'll get you. The best thing you can do is just keep on riding. Do you understand?'

'Sure thing, Marshal,' said Daniels with a broad grin and plainly very relieved. 'I'll just keep ridin' east. You won't get no trouble from me, I promise you that. I knew a girl once back in Tennessee, maybe I'll look her up.'

'You do that,' said Ellis. 'OK, you can go and just remember, you don't so much as frighten a child in this state. If you do, I'll be sure to hear about it.'

'Sure thing, Marshal, an' thanks,' said Daniels.

'Just for the record,' said Ellis, 'who are the other two who joined Saunders?'

'Luke Franks an' Josh Wellings,' said Daniels. 'The three of us were in prison with Saunders when he led the uprisin'. Neither of them is up to much, small time like me but hopin' to make it big with Saunders. Franks fancies himself as bein' fast with a gun. He might be faster'n some but he's a real slouch compared to Docherty. That's one thing you ought to remember, Marshal. As well as bein' a complete maniac, Seamus Docherty is also the fastest man on the draw I've ever seen. Not that he needs to be from what I hear.

He prefers shootin' in the back if he can.'

'Most outlaws are the same,' said Ellis. 'Including you, I expect. OK, thanks for warning me. Now get the hell out of here before I change my mind.'

'Yes, sir, Marshal Stack, sir,' said Daniels, running to his horse. 'Maybe I shouldn't say this, but I sure hope that you get Docherty before he does much more damage. He's the kind of guy who even gives outlaws a bad name.'

Ellis watched ruefully as Daniels rode away. It did rather go against all he believed in to allow an outlaw to go free, but he realized that in the present circumstances he had to swallow his pride. The important thing now was to reach Reese Pass and hope that Marshal Thomas Burns and his men were there.

Ellis reached Reese Pass rather more quickly than he had expected, arriving in the mainly tented town shortly before noon the following day. His arrival caused something of a stir, particularly amongst the miners who tended to treat any lawman with suspicion.

His reception amongst the few traders was rather more welcoming, apart from a large woman who had set up a whorehouse. Ellis had decided to ask her some questions because, in his experience, such women generally knew more about what was going on than anyone else. She explained that the arrival of a marshal invariably ended with her being forced to close down her business.

'I can't say that I approve,' said Ellis, 'but I suppose you are only supplying a need. Don't worry, I'm not here to close anyone down providing they don't break the law.'

'Then why are you here?' she asked. 'Towns like this come and go and as far as the law is concerned, we have our own. It might be rough an' ready but it works pretty well for the most part. Providin' a man don't try to jump another man's claim, steal his gold or cheat at cards, folk are left to do pretty much as they please. Claim-jumpin' an' stealin' gold normally end up with whoever it is bein' strung up from a tree. Cheatin' at cards usually ends up with the man's fingers or even hand bein' chopped off. You'll notice that nearly all the miners carry some mighty big knives just for things like that.'

'Yes, I've heard about the justice meted out by miners,' said Ellis. 'What about murder?'

'Murder's one of them things that don't happen, so I'm told,' she said. 'If a man is killed it's generally thought that he must have asked for it in some way. I don't suppose you'd agree with that though.'

'No, I wouldn't but I'm not really interested in what happens in places like this. I'm here hoping to find some prisoners who have escaped from Winnemucca. I don't suppose you've seen anyone who might be them? The one certain fact is that they are not prospectors. Have there been any strangers about during the last few days?'

'Strangers!' she said with a dry laugh. 'Sure, there's been a few. Take your pick from about two or three hundred. They come an' go all the time. Some manage to buy or win a claim at cards but most give up after a time and try their luck somewhere else. All the best claims went months ago.'

'You know what I mean,' said Ellis. 'In a place like this I imagine that anyone who isn't a prospector is fairly easy to pick out.'

'Sure, Marshal, I know exactly what you mean,' she said. 'No, sir, I'm afraid I can't help you. The last man to fit that description was through here about ten days ago, heading west. He stayed a couple of days and then just disappeared.'

'Just the one?' asked Ellis.

'Just the one,' said the woman. 'I'd say he was a drifter.'

'OK,' said Ellis. 'If any strangers do

45

come into town, I want you to let me know straight away. I've found myself a bed in that flea-pit that calls itself the Reese Pass Majestic.'

'Where there's gold you'll always find miners and fleas,' she said with a laugh. 'OK, I'll let you know.'

'Just one thing,' said Ellis. 'These men are dangerous, very dangerous. One in particular, called Seamus Docherty, will kill anyone as soon as look at them. Don't, under any circumstances, do anything to annoy any of them.'

'As long as they pay their way if they come to my place I won't upset nobody,' she said. 'How many are there?'

'Six,' said Ellis. 'There could be seven more men following them. They are a US marshal and six deputies. They've been following the others ever since they broke out of Winnemucca.'

'More lawmen!' sighed the woman, who was known as Bess. 'Pretty soon there'll be more of 'em than prospectors. Still, even marshals an' deputy marshals like a woman now an' then; they're all welcome. How about you, Marshal? I've got a couple of girls free at the moment.'

'I think I'll forgo that pleasure,' said Ellis. 'Now, is there anywhere I can get a decent meal? I'm fed up with my own cooking. Beans and dried beef lose their appeal after a couple of days. They don't provide food at the hotel'

'There's four places,' she said. 'Three of 'em ain't up to much though, nothin' but stew an' the Lord only knows what they put in it. One of 'em's run by some Chinese an' I hear that the Chinese will eat anythin' that moves or grows. I wouldn't be surprised if their stew was made up of bugs an' worms. The best place is about fifty yards down the street, right next to a big tent what's been set up as a saloon. You can't miss it. You tell Sam Walker — he runs it — that I sent you an' that he isn't to charge you the same as he charges the miners. The trouble with towns like this is that prices go through the roof.'

'Including yours?' said Ellis.

'Sure, includin' mine,' Bess admitted. 'I guess you can't blame anyone for charging as much as they can. The gold could run out and we could all be on our way tomorrow so we need to make as much money as an' when we can. If you should change your mind an' fancy one of my girls, I'll do you a special rate — five dollars. Normally it's ten.'

'Five dollars still sounds very expensive to me,' said Ellis. 'No thanks, I'm a very happily married man.'

'Even happily married men get the urge sometimes,' she said. She looked hard at him and then smiled. 'OK, Marshal, I know when I'm beaten. I'll let you know the moment any strangers come into town.'

Ellis went down the street and found Sam Walker's Eating House. There was a board outside stating what was available and the prices. The choice appeared to be between unknown meat stew, goat stew, deer stew or steak, or bear steaks, none of which really appealed to Ellis. However, he was hungry and decided that if that was what everyone else ate it could not be all that bad. He decided on a deer steak.

Sam Walker appeared genuinely pleased to see Ellis and immediately suggested that he had something which was probably a little more to his taste and would only cost five dollars instead of the usual ten dollars. It appeared that ten dollars was the going rate for most things in Reese Pass. Ellis's comment that even five dollars was still very expensive brought little response.

'Real beef steak,' said Sam Walker. 'I keep it for special customers. Fresh in two days ago. I don't get beef that often; it's too far to bring beef normally but I managed to get hold of a couple of live cows, so I know darned well just how fresh it is. You can't get much fresher than still walkin'.'

'OK, beef steak it is,' agreed Ellis. 'I'm so hungry I could eat a horse.'

'We get that too,' said Walker.

'Usually that *is* fresh, we slaughter the horses ourselves. You'd be surprised just how many horses an' mules are abandoned out here or somebody has to sell them to pay his debts.'

The meal proved remarkably good and Ellis did not really begrudge the five dollars. After he had eaten he toured the traders and more permanent residents of Reese Pass, telling them why he was there and what he expected them to do. His last call was to the assay-office where most of the gold was bought on behalf of the government.

'They could try to rob us,' said the clerk. 'It wouldn't be the first time somebody has tried it.' He indicated a large, very strong-looking safe. 'The gold's all kept in there and there isn't a stronger safe anywhere in the state.'

'What happens to the gold?' asked Ellis.

'There's a special army escort once a month,' said the clerk. 'At least twenty armed soldiers come from Fort Lovelock. There's only ever been one attempt to hold up the escort in the ten years I've been doing this job. That ended up with eight outlaws being killed.'

'So the gold is pretty safe,' said Ellis. 'Just supposing anyone did want to steal the gold, what would be the best way of going about it?'

The clerk laughed loudly. 'Only a madman would even think about it,' he said.

'One of the men I'm thinking of is mad, apparently completely mad,' Ellis said.

3

The assay-office clerk seemed quite certain that there was no way that anyone would be able to steal the gold but Ellis was not quite so sure. He did not have as much faith in the strength of the safe nor the ability of the army as the assay-office clerk had.

He also learned that the assay-office acted as a sort of bank. The value of the gold was held in credit for each prospector and paid out to him as and when he needed it or when he finally left. Everyday transactions were normally undertaken in gold which most miners kept in reserve.

The remainder of that day was uneventful and there was little that Ellis could do except wait for the arrival of either the outlaws or Marshal Burns. He did try a beer at one of the two large tents which called themselves saloons, but found the liquid completely unpalatable as well as very expensive.

There was also what was supposed to be whiskey and gin on sale, but Ellis was advised not to attempt to drink it since it was nothing more than locally produced moonshine. A fact reinforced by what were obviously stills and brewing-vats at the rear of each saloon.

However, no matter how it was made or from what, there were plenty of miners who willingly paid the exorbitant prices demanded. One of the two saloons did have what was claimed to be real Scotch whisky but the price asked for a small measure would have bought at least three full bottles elsewhere.

Early the following morning, the normal life of Reese Pass was interrupted by the arrival of two prospectors on mules leading seven horses into the town. Six of the horses had bodies across them and the seventh was ridden by a man who appeared to be injured. Ellis was immediately called on the grounds that he was a marshal and that this was plainly marshal business.

'Found 'em out at Quartz Gully,' explained one of the prospectors. 'They're all wearin' marshal's badges. It looks like they was ambushed. They're all dead barrin' one.'

Ellis went straight to the injured man, who said his name was Jim Forgan and was a deputy marshal working for Tom Burns and had been following Mitchel Saunders and his men.

'They took us from both sides,' croaked Forgan. 'We never stood a chance.'

'You can tell me exactly what happened later,' said Ellis. 'First we'd better get you seen to.' He turned to the crowd which had gathered. 'I don't suppose there's a doctor in this town?'

'Nearest we got is a man what used to be an animal doctor,' said one. 'Leastways that's what he reckons he was. He's pretty good at dealin' with gunshot wounds an' pullin' teeth.'

'Get him,' ordered Ellis.

'He's out workin' his claim,' replied the man.

'I don't care where he is,' barked Ellis. 'Get him. Can't you see this man is badly injured?'

'Yes, sir, Marshal, sir,' said the man. 'It'll take about half an hour.'

'Just get him,' ordered Ellis. 'In the meantime two of you can help me get this man to the hotel. You,' he said to another man, 'bring those horses.'

In the absence of anywhere more suitable, Jim Forgan was taken to Ellis's room, in which there was a spare bed. The wife of the owner of the hotel did her best to clean up the injuries. Although she tried her best, it was plain that she did not really know what to do next. The remaining bodies were taken to a small room at the back of the hotel. Ellis checked that they were all dead. He was able to identify the body of Marshal Tom Burns, having met the man on several occasions.

The prospector who claimed to have been an animal doctor arrived and examined Jim Forgan. He was a far younger man than Ellis had expected but he had to admit that he certainly appeared to know what he was doing.

'I think he'll live,' said Gus Deakin, the animal doctor. 'He's got about five bullets in him. He's a bit of a mess but they seem to have missed all his vital organs except perhaps the one in his chest. I think it *has* missed his heart though.'

'Can you get them out?' asked Ellis.

Gus sighed heavily. 'Now if he was a horse or somethin' I'd be puttin' him out of his misery.'

'But he isn't a horse,' said Ellis. 'This is US Deputy Marshal Jim Forgan and you don't go round puttin' folk like him, or anyone else, out of their misery.'

'It's a big job,' said Gus. 'Bigger'n anythin' I've had to tackle before. I don't know if I can. For the most part it's knife wounds, single bullets or scattergun pellets and fixin' broken bones I have to deal with. Knife wounds and shotgun pellets are easy and, although I say it myself, I do a pretty good job of settin' bones an' stitchin' a man up.'

'Isn't digging a bullet out of a man pretty much the same as digging it out of a horse?' said Ellis.

'I guess so,' admitted Gus. 'They're both made up of meat an' blood. The thing is I ain't really a qualified veterinarian. All I ever did was work for a man what was since I was twelve years old. I was goin' to go to proper veterinary school but my folks both died an' I couldn't afford it. I did learn a thing or two in the eight years I was with the veterinarian though.'

'Well, you're the only chance he has,' said Ellis.

'OK, Marshal,' said Gus. 'Just don't go holdin' me responsible if he dies. Four of the bullets shouldn't be no problem, but the other does seem pretty close to his heart. If I leave it where it is there's a good chance that he'll live. If I start cuttin' him that close to his heart, it might kill him. He really needs a proper doctor, but that's somethin' we ain't got.'

'All I ask is that you do your best,' said Ellis. 'I'll have to rely on your judgement as to whether or not to remove that bullet. You can start by taking out those you can.'

While Gus was operating, assisted by the hotel-owner's wife, Ellis went to the room where the bodies had been laid. He searched each one, gathering personal belongings in an attempt to identify them. Having gathered all the information he could, he then went to the assay-office where it was agreed that the items, including their guns, could be stored.

'Under the circumstances I think the army will take these things and the horses back to Fort Lovelock,' said the clerk. 'I expect they'll take the injured deputy as well.'

'When are they due?' asked Ellis. 'Two weeks,' said the clerk.

'Which means that the bodies will have to be buried,' said Ellis. 'They certainly won't last that long in this heat otherwise. I probably won't be here so I'll leave a letter for the commander of the escort.'

'They'd better be buried today,' said the clerk. 'One of the rules about dead bodies in places like this is that they're got rid of as soon as possible on account of rotting corpses ain't healthy.'

Ellis managed to suppress any comment but could not prevent a wry smile at the suggestion that anything should or should not be done on health grounds in a place like Reese Pass.

Later, he returned to the hotel where he found that Gus Deakin had successfully removed all but the bullet close to the deputy's heart.

'I ain't prepared to risk it,' explained Gus. 'It's a job for a proper doctor. All I can tell you is that it's about an inch above his heart. That means that while it might be uncomfortable and will have to be taken out sometime, he shouldn't die.

Bleedin' won't be no problem, I can stop that.'

'OK, I guess you've done your best,' said Ellis. 'Thanks. Any idea how long it'll be before he can walk?'

'That's up to him,' said Gus. 'He wasn't shot in the legs. He seems an otherwise pretty healthy feller. A couple of days should see him up an' about.'

'I need to talk to him,' said Ellis. 'How long will he be unconscious?'

'That I don't know,' said Gus. 'He could come round any minute now or it might be a few hours. Animals are different, they don't pass out like humans do. If an animal does pass out, you can usually say that's the end of it. I'll look in later on, but I don't think there's anythin' else I can do for him. It just needs somebody to check that some of the wounds don't go bad ways. Gangrene is the real killer out here mainly because folk don't keep things like this clean and dry.'

Jim Forgan did not recover consciousness for another half-hour. During that time Ellis questioned the two prospectors who had found the bodies. All they could tell him was that they had been out looking for places where gold might be found and were on their way back to Reese Pass when they had come across them. They had neither heard nor seen anything. They certainly had not seen any outlaws during the five days they had been prospecting.

Although he was still in some pain and rather groggy, Jim Forgan did manage to explain what had happened.

'We were closing on them,' he said. 'We knew that from the fresh tracks. We came to this gully and at first Tom — that's Marshal Tom Burns — was very reluctant to go through it. He said he had an uneasy feelin' about the gully. We tried to find a way round but it was just impossible. Tom really didn't have any alternative and ordered us into the gully. Don't go thinkin' it was because he got things wrong; Tom Burns didn't get things wrong. He told us what he thought might happen. We were about three or four hundred yards in when they suddenly opened up on us from both sides. There was nothin' we could do, the sides of the gully were maybe thirty feet high an' they'd climbed up an' were above us. There was just nowhere any of us could take cover. Tom was the first to fall, I saw that plain enough. After that all hell broke loose.'

'How did you manage to survive?' asked Ellis. 'I would have thought they would have made certain that you were all dead. I've examined the bodies and it looks to me as though two of the others were shot in the head after they'd fallen. I've seen things like that before and know when a bullet has been fired from close range or not.'

'Darned if I know,' said Forgan. 'All I remember is feelin' a couple of bullets an' then everythin' went black. I came round just before those prospectors found us. Mitch Saunders must have assumed I was dead. All I know is it happened just before sunset.'

'You were lucky,' said Ellis. 'I gather this Quartz Gully is about five miles from here and there's no other way anyone can go either in or out of Reese Pass. The one thing I am quite certain of is that Saunders and his men did not come here. Have you any idea where they might have gone?'

'No,' croaked Forgan. 'I don't know a thing before the prospectors found me. I know Tom was rather surprised when they headed for Reese Pass in the first place though. I ain't sure how, but he seemed to know they were after gold. He reckoned that they must've known how many miners there are here and about the assay-office. He reckoned it was probably harder to get gold out of here than the state treasury. He was expectin' them to head for that other town what's sprung up further south where there isn't an assay-office. I can't remember what it's called. He said the miners there would be fairly easy to rob.'

'I hear it's called Mud City,' said Ellis. 'That would make more sense. I gather there's only about three hundred miners and, as you say, no assay office. I wonder why they didn't head that way in the first place?'

'Mud City!' said Forgan with a rather painful laugh. 'Mud, out here?'

'That's what they told me back in Eureka,' said Ellis. 'There's supposed to be so much mud about that they called it Mud City. I suppose there are times of the year when it could be like that.'

'If they say so,' said Forgan. 'Sorry I can't be of more help, Marshal. Tom said we'd probably meet up with you. You are Marshal Ellis Stack? I heard about you, you've got quite a reputation.'

'A reputation is something I could well do without,' said Ellis. 'I've seen what reputations can do to people. Men like you and me who do have a reputation tend to attract every no-good who thinks he has to prove he's faster on the draw than anyone else and you in particular. OK, I'll leave you to get some rest. I need to think about my next move. I have to arrange for the bodies to be buried as well. It seems that there is no room for ceremony in this part of the world.'

'I might be wrong, Marshal,' said Forgan, 'but I reckon Saunders led us to that gully quite deliberately. Up to then there hadn't really been anywhere they could have ambushed us. I think he did what he had to do and then headed off for this Mud City place. Just one thing. Tom reckoned there was only six of 'em but we know they started off from Rochester seven strong.'

'I know,' said Ellis. 'I met up with a man named Joe Daniels. He started off with them at Rochester but claimed that he couldn't stand Seamus Docherty any longer, especially after he was supposed to have murdered a woman at some farm.'

'He did, or at least one of them did,' said Forgan. 'We found the bodies. God knows what they did to that woman, she certainly wasn't a pretty sight when they'd finished with her. We found her stark naked, knifed in the belly and shot in her head. The man had been shot in his chest. I don't think he'd been dead too long when we found him. Talkin' of bodies. I take it all the others *are* dead? I know you said something about arranging burials.'

'Unfortunately, yes,' said Ellis. 'I'm arranging for the army escort that collects gold from the assay-office to take you and all their belongings back to Fort Lovelock. I expect you know where that is. It'll be about two weeks before they get here though and I can't afford to wait that long. The bodies will have to buried out here. If you're right about Mud City being the real target I need to get there as soon as I can.'

The bodies were buried without ceremony later that morning. Apart from a couple of would-be prospectors who had no claims and whom Ellis paid to dig the graves, himself, the hotel owner and his wife and, surprisingly, Gus Deakin, who had helped a very insistent Jim Forgan to the gravesides, there were no other witnesses. They could hardly be called mourners since death was almost an everyday occurrence and, for the most part, the deceased completely anonymous.

Ellis then decided to ride out to Quartz Gully to see if he could make out which way Saunders and his men had gone. Finding Quartz Gully was easy. Gus Deakin had told him that there was no mistaking it. It was apparently about a mile long, perhaps fifty feet wide at its widest and with sheer walls varying from about thirty feet to over fifty feet to a narrow ledge and then rising perhaps another three or four hundred feet. He had also been told that it was impossible to use the ledge since this completely disappeared in a few places.

He easily found the place where the ambush had occured; there were still some bloodstains. There were clear signs, plainly recent, of horses leading away from the scene and away from Reese Pass. He followed these tracks beyond the gully and found that they departed from the main trail after about a mile. They appeared to have taken a generally southerly direction. He followed them for a short distance just to make certain that they were heading south. He then decided to return to Reese Pass.

News of the murder of Marshal Tom Burns and his deputies had spread rapidly through the community and immediately on his return Ellis was bombarded with questions. Most seemed rather less concerned that a few lawmen had been murdered than they were about their own safety. All Ellis could tell them was that the killers had apparently headed south, over the mountains. The comment quite often repeated was that only a madman would try to cross the mountains. He did not mention the fact that one of them was mad.

As was quite normal in such circumstances, the number of men involved increased at each telling. At least twenty desperadoes were now known to have been involved. Ellis made no attempt to tell them otherwise but his silence simply served to fuel speculation.

The condition of Jim Forgan seemed to have improved even in the short time Ellis had been away. He was even talking of going with Ellis to Mud City, but Ellis had to make it quite plain that he was in no condition to travel anywhere just yet. He did not say that he preferred to work alone.

'There's still a bullet lodged close to your heart,' he said. 'You need to get to a doctor as quick as possible. If I had the time I'd take you myself, but I have to find Saunders before he kills anyone else.'

'In other words you don't want a cripple with you,' said Forgan, rather bitterly. 'They were my friends, Marshal. Three of us had been together for over four years. I want their killers.'

'And revenge is the worst motive for wanting to get Saunders,' said Ellis.

'You ought to know that. Revenge makes you do things you wouldn't normally do, take chances and, more importantly, makes you lose sight of the real objective. I've seen it before. A good lawman turned into nothing better than the men he was after because he was out for revenge. Sorry, Jim, I go alone.'

Forgan tried pleading with Ellis but he remained adamant. He wrote a letter to the commander of the army unit due in two weeks, left it with the assay-office and instructed Gus Deakin to keep an eye on the deputy. He rode out of Reese Pass the following morning and headed south.

★　★　★

He had been told that all he had to do to find Mud City was to follow the Reese River south, something which proved to be easier said than done. At several points the river ran through steep-sided gorges and he was forced to make several detours although he always managed to find the river again. His only real difficulty came when he came across another river, running into the Reese River and which seemed to be larger. Since this river came from a more westerly direction, he crossed it and hoped that he was still following the Reese River.

At about midday on his second day, Ellis came across a small group of men who were plainly prospectors. They confirmed that he was still heading in the correct direction for Mud City.

'You'll probably reach it in another two days,' said one of them. 'It's taken us almost four days to get this far, but we've only got mules. It should be quicker on a horse. We've come from there but decided to try our luck in Reese Pass.'

'I think there's more than three thousand miners there,' said Ellis. 'Claims can be pretty hard to come by. I know there's plenty of men without claims.'

'It's allus the same,' said one of the others, rather ruefully. 'Mud City ain't so big but all the best claims have gone. What the hell brings a US marshal out here? Normally the law don't want to know about folk like us.'

'You probably left Mud City at the right time,' said Ellis. 'If my information is correct, there's a bunch of escaped prisoners headin' that way right now.'

'Mitch Saunders,' said another man. 'Sure, we heard about that. We should've guessed that's why you're here. We also heard that they was headin' for Reese Pass.'

'How the hell did you know about him?' asked Ellis.

'You'd be surprised how quickly word spreads out here,' replied the man. 'Folk seem to know what's happenin' almost before it happens.'

'I'm past being surprised,' said Ellis. 'I'm just curious as to why you decided to go to Reese Pass knowin' that they had gone that way. If your information was that good you would have known these are very dangerous men.'

'Truth is somebody met a man who was with Saunders,' said one. 'It was him what said they was headed for Reese Pass.'

'Joe Daniels, I met him too,' said Ellis. 'Unfortunately I had to let him go.'

'More important things to do,' said another. 'We reckon Mud City is just about worked out. Folk like us have to go where the gold is an' Reese Pass is where it's at at the moment. We figured that Mitch Saunders an' his men would be long gone by the time we reached there. Leastways that's what we'd hoped. Anyway, there ain't nowhere else to go at the moment.' '

'Well they never even reached there,' said Ellis. 'They ambushed and murdered another US marshal and five of his deputies not far from the town and then headed south towards Mud City. You should be safe enough but I don't rate your chances of stakin' a claim as very high.'

'That's a chance we'll have to take,' the man replied. 'We gets by an' we'll strike it rich one day, I can feel it in my bones.'

'Then I wish you the best of luck,' said Ellis. 'Is this Mud City as muddy as they say it is?'

'I've seen worse,' said one of the men. 'The biggest problem is water runnin' off the mountains. We've seen a few claims completely buried in mud after even a light fall of rain. Them mountains seem to attract rain. It can be dry as a bone down in the valley but rainin' like hell a few hundred feet up in the mountains.'

'And Reese Pass seems to be nothin' but rock,' said Ellis. 'I know a few prospectors do strike it lucky, but it seems a hard way to make a livin' to me.'

'Almost as bad as tryin' to arrest outlaws,' said one of them. 'Each to his own, Marshal. I don't think any of us would choose to do what you do. At least we live in the hope of becoming rich one day, all you've got to look forward to is a bullet in the back or failin' that a few dollars' pension to live on, if you're lucky. I know, my brother-in-law is a sheriff.'

'You have a point, I suppose,' said Ellis.

Two days later, Ellis found himself on top of a hill, spyglass in hand, studying a hotchpotch of tents at the base of some steep hills. He had no doubt that he had reached Mud City. From where he was, about a mile away, it was impossible to tell if Mud City lived up to its name.

The indications were that life in Mud City was pretty much that which might be expected. There was certainly no sign of the outlaws but his gut feeling was that they were not too far away. He decided to remain where he was for the moment and study the comings and goings of the town.

There was only one building constructed of timber as far as he could see and, judging by the number of and frequency with which people visited the place, he had to assume that it was either a saloon or a whore-house or probably even both. Whores and alcohol were invariably amongst the early arrivals at any gold strike.

The remainder of that day passed without incident and Ellis decided to stay where he was until the following morning. As darkness descended, oil-lamps and fires appeared, giving the impression that the town was larger than it actually was.

He spent the first two hours after daybreak once again studying the town through his spyglass. After about the first hour there appeared to be a flurry of activity with several men rushing from tent to tent and pointing up a narrow valley behind the town.

His instinct was to ride down to Mud City and find out what was going on but he resisted and kept watch for another hour. During that time a large group of miners appeared and he could just make out two bodies thrown across the back of a mule. He had the feeling that he knew exactly what had happened.

There were other possibilities of course. It was possible that the men had been discovered stealing from someone's claim and had been on the receiving end of summary justice, or it was equally possible that there had been an accident of some kind.

He knew that accidents were not at all uncommon, with men falling or mine shafts collapsing. On this occasion, however, there was, in his opinion, rather more fuss being made of it than would be expected if it had been an accident.

He packed up his few belongings and rode down to Mud City.

4

As far as Ellis was aware, there had been no rain for at least a week. There had certainly been no sign of recent rains between Reese Pass and Mud City. However, as he approached Mud City, he quickly discovered just why it had been given that name.

Even well before reaching the tented town, the ground underfoot became distinctly soft and wet. The obviously well-used track along which he was riding was surrounded by a wide marsh.

As he drew nearer to the town he could see numerous small streams running off the mountain and into the marsh. The town itself was set on slightly higher and apparently firmer ground, but there was still no shortage of mud.

A small stream ran through the

centre which, from the edge of the town down as far as the marsh, seemed to be little more than an open sewer. Litter and waste of almost every description lay in and around the stream. The stench was almost overpowering and numerous rats scuttled out of his way as he approached.

His arrival, as ever in places such as this, was greeted with total silence and obvious distrust. His badge of office plainly did not go unnoticed. He made his way to where he had last seen the bodies being offloaded from the mule.

'Mornin',' he said to a rather large man whose dress was definitely not in keeping with that of being a prospector. 'United States Marshal Ellis Stack,' he continued by way of introduction. 'It looks like you've been having a bit of trouble.'

'Who says so?' grunted the man.

'I've been observing you from back there,' said Ellis. 'I saw a couple of bodies bein' brought into town. From the way everyone was acting it certainly didn't seem as though it was a normal accident.'

'It's nothing we can't handle,' said the man, obviously rather better educated than the average prospector. 'A marshal, you say?' he continued. 'Now what possible business could bring a man like you out here? I think you must have the wrong place; you must be looking for Reese Pass.'

'This *is* Mud City?' said Ellis. The man nodded. 'Then I do have the right place,' continued Ellis. 'If my guess is right, I think that you have just found out why I am here. What happened to those men?'

'Since you seem to know all about what's going on here, you tell me,' replied the man.

Ellis dismounted and tethered his horse to a nearby hitching rail before speaking.

'I think those men were shot, murdered,' he said. 'I don't think it was one of your local disputes either. The reason I am here is to try and arrest some outlaws who I'm pretty certain are in the area. Four of them escaped from prison in Winnemucca and two more joined them in Rochester. I also believe that you have a very good idea what I am talking about. I'd like to see the bodies.'

'In that tent over there,' said the man. 'They'll be buried this afternoon.'

Ellis went to the tent and looked at the bodies. The injuries were much as he had expected.

By that time quite a crowd of inquisitive prospectors had gathered round. The man nodded and indicated that Ellis should follow him. Ellis was not surprised when the man led him to the only wooden building in Mud City, consisting of two rather flimsy-looking storeys. As expected, the building turned out to be a bar. There were also several girls drinking with what few customers there were.

'I'm Vincent Parkes,' said the man as he led Ellis to a small room off the main saloon. 'I have the doubtful privilege of being the owner of this establishment. I am also a judge, authorized by the state.'

'A judge?' queried Ellis. 'You're the first judge I've ever met who also owns a bar and a whorehouse. Do you have any proof of your status?'

'Right here,' said the judge, opening a drawer in a desk. He handed a paper to Ellis. 'I am also licensed to perform marriages, register claims and act in cases of disputes.'

'So I see,' said Ellis, reading the document. 'Do you have much call for presiding at weddings?'

'I've only done one in the past three months,' said Parkes. 'The thing is, I'm the law round here and I don't like anyone interfering.'

'I have no intention of interfering in anything,' said Ellis. 'I have more than enough problems of my own without taking on places like this. My business is to apprehend the outlaws I mentioned. Now, was my first guess right or not?'

'It was,' conceded Parkes. 'Those two men were discovered on their claim. Both have been shot and it looks as though they were robbed of their gold. I have no idea how much that was but I heard that they had struck a good seam.'

'And it wasn't another prospector claim-jumping or stealing the gold?' said Ellis. Parkes shook his head. 'You might have the authority for dealing with purely local matters,' Ellis continued, 'but escaped convicts are my business. I see that your authority is confined to Mud City, Reese Pass and all the territory between Reese Pass and Mud City and lying between the Shoshone Mountains and the Toiyabe mountains. Why Reese Pass?'

'It seemed a good idea, that's all,' said Parkes. 'I might have to close up and go to Reese Pass.'

'They've already got a couple of saloons and cathouses but I don't think they have a judge,' said Ellis. 'Still, it's nice to know that there is some kind of law round here. I had hoped to reach here before things like this happened. You are aware of just who these men are?'

'Word has it that they are Mitchel Saunders, Lefty Swann, Jim Coburn and Seamus Docherty,' said Parkes. 'At least they are the ones who are supposed to have broken out of prison.'

'Correct,' said Ellis. 'You obviously heard that from a man named Joe Daniels, who is also a wanted outlaw.'

'He didn't come here,' said Parkes, defensively. 'A couple of prospectors met him up in the mountains. We heard that they were heading for Reese Pass.'

'Of course, as a judge, you would have had Daniels arrested had he come here,' said Ellis. Parkes remained silent. 'No matter,' Ellis continued. 'I must confess to having allowed Daniels to go free myself. I simply didn't have the time to deal with him. Yes, they did almost reach Reese Pass but that appears to have been nothing more than a trap. They murdered another US marshal and five of his deputies who were on their tail at a place called Quartz Gully. After they'd murdered them, they headed this way which, I am now certain, was their original plan. They are after gold and Reese Pass is not an easy place to get it because most of it is kept at the assay-office.'

'Murdered a marshal?' queried Parkes. 'I guess that does take things out of my hands. You think that the killing of those two prospectors and the escaped prisoners are tied up? We do get a few saddlebums through here from time to time and they have been known to steal gold.'

'Have there been any through lately?' asked Ellis.

'No, guess not,' admitted Parkes. 'OK, Mr Stack, sorry about the way I greeted you, but I didn't know exactly why you were here. I certainly didn't know about the marshal and his men being killed. If there is anything I can do to help, you just let me know.'

'Do you have much influence round here?' asked Ellis.

'I am a judge!' said Parkes.

'Perhaps you are,' said Ellis. 'That isn't quite the same thing. For instance, could you organize the miners into some sort of fighting force. It might be necessary to do just that.'

'Against hardened gunfighters such as Saunders and Docherty are supposed to be?' asked Parkes. 'Marshal, these men are prospectors, miners, they're used to hard work but they are more used to picks and shovels than to guns. In fact I don't think there are many of them who have decent guns. Most disputes are settled with knives. Mainly card-cheats.'

'So I hear,' said Ellis. 'Are there many men walking about with fingers missing? They tell me a man caught cheating at cards usually has his fingers chopped off.'

'There's a few,' admitted Parkes. 'Usually they're greenhorns, a few gamblers and some fools who think all miners are stupid. The greenhorns and fools usually lose a couple of fingers at first, just as a warning. They don't normally cheat after that. If you see a man walking around with no hand, you can guarantee he's a gambler who's also stupid. We don't get many of them though. Most gamblers know they'll win in the long run.'

'And, as a judge, you allow this form of justice?' said Ellis. 'It works,' shrugged Parkes.

'And what happens to claim-jumpers or men stealing gold?'

'We hang them,' said Parkes. 'After a fair trial of course. We try them in the morning and hang them in the afternoon. That works pretty well too.'

'I must admit that it seems to,' agreed Ellis. 'I saw plenty of knives in Reese Pass but I didn't see that many guns. It looks the same here.'

'Most of them have shotguns,' said Parkes. 'They're more use than rifles when it comes to hunting small game and they can give a man a mighty sore ass when he gets a blast up him. There are a few with rifles but I think you'll find they're mostly muzzle-loaders. If a man does have a handgun you can bet your life that he's either stolen it or found it somewhere. Prospectors don't like wasting their money on things like that.'

'Muzzle-loading rifles?' queried Ellis. 'I'm surprised they're still in use.'

'They're cheaper than a modern rifle,' said Parkes. 'Ammunition is the thing that really costs and is hard to get hold of, so most of them buy an old muzzle-loader and then make their own bullets. Lead and gunpowder are easy enough to come by. They're used mainly for hunting things like goats and deer.'

'I suppose it makes sense,' said Ellis. 'OK, we've sorted out who you are and why I am here. The next question is can you rent me a room?'

'I don't normally rent out rooms,' said Parkes. 'Under the circumstances though, I reckon I can find one. Will that be with or without a girl?'

'Without,' said Ellis. 'I'm right off

luxuries at the moment.'

'Then how does ten dollars a week sound?'

'It sounds mighty expensive, unless that includes food,' said Ellis. 'I hope I'm not here a week.'

'The food isn't up to much, nothing like you're used to I expect,' said Parkes. 'Mostly it's stew of some kind but we sell quite a bit of it. Very often it isn't wise to ask exactly what it is. I leave that kind of thing up to my cook, he's Chinese and pretends he doesn't understand much English. I know he understands every word though, so it's better to watch what you're saying when he's around.'

'I dare say I've eaten worse,' said Ellis.

'OK, then, ten dollars includin' breakfast an' dinner it is,' agreed Parkes. 'If you want a girl that'll be extra. That'll be ten dollars in advance.'

'Don't you trust me to pay?' asked Ellis.

'Marshal, I've been doing this kind of

thing for a long time. Too long I think sometimes,' said Parkes. 'I trust nobody, not even US marshals. I was in a place called Yellow River Bend a couple of years ago and we had another marshal come into town. I trusted him to pay me when he left, but one day he just upped and went. I never did get my money.'

'OK, ten dollars in advance,' said Ellis, taking the money from his pocket. 'Now, I want to know where these men had their claim and their names.'

'About two miles out of town,' said the judge. 'Out at a place called McFee's Basin. Some feller named Angus McFee found gold out there about twelve months ago. That was more or less the start of the gold-rush round here. They were Tom Smith and Clayton Palmer. I think Smith was his real name but a good many don't use their real names and Smith, Jones or Brown are the most common.'

'Is this Angus McFee still around?'

'He died six months ago,' said the judge. 'It wasn't what you're probably thinking; he died of pneumonia.'

'You have a doctor then?' asked Ellis.

'Not now, but six months ago we did,' replied Parkes. 'He died too, fell off his horse when he was drunk and broke his neck. Even a prospector can tell a broken neck when he sees one. Since then any medical problems have been dealt with by one of my girls who claims that her father was a doctor. She seems pretty good but mostly it's broken bones, knife-wounds and the occasional gunshot-wound she has to deal with. Anything more serious and whoever it is has to go elsewhere or just hope that they get over it.'

'This McFee's Basin,' said Ellis, 'are there any other prospectors up there?'

'There's three other claims,' said Parkes. 'It was one of them who found Smith and Palmer. They say that they never heard a thing.'

'If they were shot I would have thought gunfire would have been easy to hear,' said Ellis. 'Perhaps I'd better have words with them.'

'They're still in town,' said Parkes. 'In fact they're in the bar right now.'

'Then I'll talk to them in here, if that's OK?'

'Do I have a choice?' muttered the judge. 'I'll send them in.'

Jimmy Grover and Amos Hutchinson, both middle-aged men, came into the room and were plainly worried about being summoned by the marshal. They both removed their hats and stood before Ellis, nervously twiddling with the brims. They licked their lips and shuffled their feet in anticipation as they introduced themselves in turn.

'We didn't do nothin',' said Grover defensively even before being asked any questions. 'We just found 'em.'

'Nobody is trying to say that you did do anything,' said Ellis. 'All I want to know is what happened.'

'How the hell do we know that?' croaked Hutchinson. 'We found 'em, that's all. We was comin' into town an' had to pass through their claim. That's when we found 'em. They was just lyin' by their tent. Anybody could see they'd been shot. The guns we've got are only shotguns an' they don't make holes in a man like that. Mind, if they're fired close to they can blow a man's head off.'

'I know, I've seen it before. Don't worry, I'm not accusing you of anything. I know who did it.'

'Just settin' the record straight, Marshal,' said Hutchinson.

'Consider it straight,' said Ellis. 'How far from their claim is yours?'

'McFee's Basin is maybe two miles or more wide,' said Hutchinson. 'Our claim is at the far end from here an' Tom an' Clay's claim was closest to town, so I guess that makes us somethin' over two miles apart.'

'I hear there's two other claims being worked,' said Ellis. 'Where are they?'

Jimmy Grover leant forward and drew a circle in the dust on the desk.

'Our place is here,' he marked a cross on the circle. 'Tom an' Clay's is here,' he marked another cross almost oppo-site. 'Sam Benthall an' Josh Brown's is here,' he marked another cross almost midway round the circle. 'An' this one is Cagney's. He works it by himself.' He marked another cross.

'I see,' said Ellis. 'So, looking at it like a clock-face, you are at twelve o'clock, Benthall and Brown are at three o'clock, Smith and Palmer at six o'clock and Cagney at nine o'clock.'

'Couldn't've put it better myself,' said Hutchinson. 'There's maybe somethin' over a mile between each claim at least.'

'Even so,' said Ellis, 'in my experience the sound of gunfire travels a long way. Are you quite certain you didn't hear or see anything? It could be important. You are aware just who the murderers are? They're very dangerous men and are best left alone.'

'We didn't hear nothin',' said Grover. 'They reckon it's some prisoners what escaped from Winnemucca. Is that why you're here?'

'It is,' said Ellis, 'so don't worry, I'm not interested in any of your local disputes providing it doesn't involve murder. Now, Judge Parkes has told me that it appears that Smith and Palmer were robbed. I'm curious, how does he know that?'

Jimmy Grover glanced nervously at his companion and licked his lips. 'We searched,' he said. 'We looked in all the usual places but couldn't find no gold.'

'The usual places?' queried Ellis.

'Sure,' said Hutchinson. 'We all got places where we hide our gold. There ain't no assay-office or bank in Mud City so each man has to look after his own gold. We know Tom an' Clay hit it pretty big a couple of weeks ago so there must've been some gold hidden somewhere.'

'That's right,' said Grover. 'I guess we all like to think that nobody would be able to find the gold but we all know really that it don't take that much findin'.'

'Such as?' prompted Ellis.

'Oh, you know,' said Grover. 'Under a special rock, in a mine-shaft if there is one, in a hole under the tent or even in a leather pouch under a rock in the stream. You know the kind of place. Most folk have their own special places but after a time you get to know the most likely.'

'And you searched all the likely places?' asked Ellis. 'Tell me, why did you search first and bring the bodies in later?'

'On account of if we hadn't looked someone else was sure to,' said Hutchinson.

'Of course, if you had found the gold you would have brought it into town and handed it to Judge Parkes,' said Ellis, sarcastically. His sarcasm appeared lost on the two men as they both nodded eagerly.

'Sure thing,' said Hutchinson. 'That'd be the only decent thing to do so's it could be passed on to their next of kin.'

'Very civic-minded of you,' said Ellis. 'So, if you didn't find any gold then the likelihood is that it was stolen by the outlaws. Of course it is possible that they didn't find it either in which case I had better check. I think the outlaws did get hold of it though. Smith and Palmer were killed cleanly so they must have handed it over or told them where it was. If they hadn't I am quite certain they would have tortured those men until they did, but there's no sign of torture. Did you see any sign that a search had been made?'

'Nothin' at all,' said Hutchinson. 'Only thing we saw was signs that a few horses had been there, that's all.'

'How many horses?' asked Ellis.

'How the hell are we supposed to know things like that?' asked Grover. 'All we can say is that there was quite a few of 'em. We're prospectors, not trackers. Maybe Apache Joe can tell you. He's an Indian what's turned to tryin' his luck diggin' for gold. Like most Indians though, he drinks everythin' he finds.'

'He might be useful,' said Ellis. 'Where can I find him?'

'Right now, in the bar,' said Grover. 'He shouldn't be in there, we know that an' Vince knows it too. It's against the law to supply Indians with drink but he turns a blind eye since Apache Joe is the only Indian round here an' he does spend all his gold in here.'

'I'm not interested in things like that,' said Ellis. 'I wonder, gentlemen, would you mind turning out your pockets?'

'What for?' demanded Hutchinson. 'You accusin' us of stealin' the gold?'

'No, I am not,' said Ellis. 'I am simply eliminating the possibility. Of course, I can't force you to turn out your pockets, but if you have nothing to hide I see little reason for you to refuse.'

'All we got with us is about an ounce,' said Grover. 'We've got more but it's safely hidden away.'

'I have no idea how much an ounce of gold is worth,' said Ellis, 'but it doesn't sound much to me. I suppose an ounce can buy you almost everything you need in a place like this.'

'It's enough to get by on,' said Grover. 'OK, Marshal, we'll turn out our pockets but I must register my objection. We're both honest men an' don't steal nothin' off nobody.'

'You can take it up with the appropriate authority,' said Ellis.

The men turned out their pockets and laid the contents on the desk. There were two lengths of twine each about a foot long, an old tinder-box, two tins each containing several whole cheroots and even more partly smoked, two pocket-knives, a lump of what looked like chalk, a well-worn pencil-stub, thirty-two cents in coin and a small leather pouch. Ellis opened the pouch and saw that it did contain a small amount of gold. Seemingly satisfied, he told the men to put the things back in their pockets.

'Thank you, gentlemen,' he said. 'Sorry to make it appear that I didn't believe you, but I had to be certain. I hear that some men will go to great lengths to get their hands on gold.'

'I guess so, Marshal,' grunted Hutchinson. 'Can we go now?'

'I don't see why not,' said Ellis. 'I might be along to take a look at your claim sometime.'

'I would've thought you'd be more interested in findin' them outlaws what murdered Tom an' Clay,' muttered Grover.

'I am,' said Ellis. 'But the thought had crossed my mind that you and the others out at McFee's Basin might be next on the list for being robbed and murdered. I certainly wouldn't like that to happen.'

'Neither would we,' grunted Hutchinson. 'OK Marshal, I guess you is only doin' your job. I hope you find 'em before they kill anyone else.'

'I shall try to, Mr Hutchinson,' said Ellis. 'I shall certainly try. If this Apache Joe is in the bar, send him in will you?'

'He's probably blind drunk by now,' said Grover.

'I shall just have to take that chance,' said Ellis. 'Thank you for being so helpful.'

5

Contrary to expectations, Apache Joe did not appear the worse for drink. He came into the office and eyed Ellis warily, obviously expecting to be told that he should not be drinking in the bar. He was a thin, middle-aged man, rather taller than most Indians Ellis had met.

'Mr Parkes allows me to drink in the bar,' said the Indian, defensively.

'I am not interested in that,' said Ellis. 'Your drinking habits are nothing to do with me.'

'Then why do you call me?' he asked.

'I'm told you might be a good tracker,' said Ellis. 'I need a man to help me. It's something I'm not very good at.'

'Because I am Apache everybody thinks I must be a good tracker,' replied the Indian.'

'Well are you?' asked Ellis. 'I must admit that most Indians I have ever met seem to have been born with such skills.'

'I still remember many of the old ways,' replied Joe. 'It is not something that is easily forgotten. I worked for the army for a few years as a tracker. They gave me the rank of sergeant.'

'Which makes you just the man I need,' said Ellis. 'I have no doubt that you know why I am here but just in case you don't, I will explain. You must know that two prospectors were murdered and their gold stolen.' The Indian nodded. 'I believe that the men who did it are a bunch of outlaws.' continued Ellis. 'Four of them escaped from prison at Winnemucca. I have been sent to take them back to prison. They have already killed eight people, two out at a remote farm and then another US marshal and five deputies.'

'That is what I have heard,' confirmed Joe.

'Now they appear to have murdered

two more and unless I get them soon there's likely to be a few more murders,' said Ellis. 'I must admit that my tracking skills are not all that good, which is why I need someone like you.'

'I have a claim to work,' said Joe. 'How can I help you and find gold?'

'All the gold in the world is no use to a dead man,' said Ellis. 'There's no knowing where they will strike next, it might even be you.'

'I can look after myself,' said Joe.

'I have no doubt that you can,' said Ellis. 'Aren't you bothered what happens to the other miners?'

'They do not care about me, so why should I care about them,' said Joe. 'Sometimes they find me useful when it comes to tracking goats or deer but when I need help they do not want to know me.'

'Then you will not help?' said Ellis.

'I did not say that, Marshal,' said Joe. 'Tom Smith and Clayton Palmer were among the few who did offer to help me. If I do help you find these men, it will not be for the others, it will be because they were my friends.'

'That's as good a reason as any,' said Ellis. 'Will you ride out with me to McFee's Basin?'

'Now?' asked Joe.

'There's no point in wasting time,' said Ellis. 'I would imagine that fairly fresh tracks are easier to follow.'

'I was paid for tracking with the army,' said Joe. 'Will you also pay me? While I am working for you I cannot find gold.'

Ellis sighed. He had been expecting this. 'I can't afford to pay you much but I suppose I could find the price of a couple of bottles of whiskey.'

'For three bottles I will help,' said Joe.

'Then we have a deal,' said Ellis. 'I take it you have a horse or a mule, do you have a gun?'

'I have a Winchester rifle,' said Joe, proudly. 'I took it with me when the army no longer needed me. I am the only one in Mud City with such a gun and there are many who would like to take it off me. I also have ammunition.'

'Do you have it with you?' asked Ellis.

'It is not wise to carry such a weapon when it is not needed,' said Joe. 'It is hidden on my claim. Some have searched for it but never found it. I must first go and get it. I will go now and return here.'

'I'll come with you if you like,' offered Ellis.

'No, I will go by myself,' insisted Joe. 'I will return in half an hour.'

Ellis shrugged and allowed Apache Joe to go. He could well understand the reason why he did not want anyone to see where he kept his rifle. There were many men, prospectors and miners amongst them, who would go to almost any length to get their hands on a Winchester rifle.

Less than half an hour later Apache Joe returned and, surprisingly, he was riding a horse. Ellis had expected the usual mule.

'I don't know where this McFee's Basin is,' said Ellis as he mounted his horse. 'You'll have to lead the way.'

'It is not far,' said Joe. 'There is only one track, it is impossible to get lost.'

'I can get myself lost coming out of a door,' said Ellis, laughing. 'Lead on.'

It took them about half an hour to reach McFee's Basin and Smith and Palmer's claim. Ellis could see why it had been called a basin. It was, as he had expected, a large, almost circular depression surrounded by mountains and appeared to be about two miles across at any one point. The floor of it was littered with boulders of various sizes with a few trees scattered around.

Smith and Palmer's claim was set slightly off the main track alongside a small but fast-flowing stream. There were all the usual items associated with gold-workings: a rickety-looking sluice and riddle, an equally decrepit-looking wheelbarrow and several picks and shovels. There were a few cooking utensils alongside the remains of a fire.

The tent was still there and, out of little more than curiosity, Ellis looked inside but found nothing more than some dirty blankets.

'First thing we have to do is make sure that their gold *was* stolen,' said Ellis looking around and plainly lost as to where to start.

'There is no shaft,' said Joe. 'All we can do is look under some rocks or in the water. A lot of men hide their gold in a leather pouch in the water. I will look there, you look under some of the rocks.'

It did not take long for Apache Joe to declare that there was no gold.

'How about men and horses?' asked Ellis. 'It all looks pretty messy to me but even I can see that there have been a few horses and things about.'

Apache Joe spent some time examining the ground, particularly on the approaches to the site. Eventually he declared that at least five men and their horses had been there and that when they had left they had made their way down into the basin.

'These tracks here,' said Joe, pointing at a jumble of marks on the ground. 'These are mule. I do not think that these men ride mules so they can be ignored. These,' he said pointing at some other tracks, 'they are made by horses. Also, one of the men has boots which are badly worn and he has big feet.'

'Can you follow the tracks?' asked Ellis.

'The signs are clear,' said Joe. 'You wish me to follow them now?'

'Let's see which way they're headed,' said Ellis 'We've got a few hours daylight left. I have the feeling that they won't be too far away.'

At first the tracks led down into the basin before turning off and up the quite steep sides. As they made their way up the sides, Joe pointed to a flat area with a good view where, he claimed, the men had stopped for a while but had not dismounted.

Ellis looked out across the basin. In

the centre, previously out of sight, was a small lake. There appeared to be a river running out of it towards the northern side of the basin. About a quarter of a mile away and slightly to his right, there were clear signs of one of the other claims, although there was no sign of life other than a mule. Ellis took out his spyglass and studied the area more closely.

'I don't like it,' he said as he put his spyglass away. 'It's too quiet down there. There has to be somebody about because of the mule, but I don't see anybody.'

'Then we must look,' said Joe. 'I think this claim belongs to Sam Benthall and Josh Brown. I did not see them in town.'

'We'd better,' agreed Ellis. 'Even if they are there, they might not have heard what happened.'

As they made their way down, Joe announced that the men they were following had also gone that way. He pointed out tracks to Ellis who simply grunted and said that he took the Indian's word for it.

They reached the workings and at first there was no sign of anyone or anything other than the mule. They dismounted and, rifles in hand, started to search. It did not take long for Joe to call Ellis.

'In here,' said Joe, pointing at a mine shaft. 'They are dead.'

Ellis had to walk into the shaft almost doubled up and the light gradually disappeared. However, there was still enough light to enable Ellis to see two bodies. He bent down to examine them but there was no doubting Joe's statement that they were dead. Their clothes were soaked in blood and each had wounds to their heads and in various other parts of their bodies.

'Let's get them out,' said Ellis.

When they had dragged the bodies out, Ellis examined them more closely. The fatal wounds were plainly the shots to their heads.

'It seems to me that they had to be

persuaded to talk,' said Joe. 'We must look for any gold.'

'At least six other shots in each body,' said Ellis. 'Somehow I don't think we're going to find any gold. Still, we'd better look I suppose.'

As expected, they were unable to find any gold apart from a small amount in a leather pouch in the pocket of one of the men.

'I think that they must have told where the rest of the gold was,' said Joe. 'Two days ago Josh Brown was saying that they now had almost enough to retire on.'

'Well they won't be retiring now,' said Ellis. 'OK, let's load them on the mule and get them back to town.'

'First I will see which way the killers went,' said Joe.

The Indian left Ellis to struggle with the bodies while he disappeared up the hill. Ten minutes later he returned and told Ellis that the tracks led out of the basin and up into the hills.

'Will you be able to follow them?' asked Ellis.

'They make no effort to hide their tracks,' said Joe. 'It will be easy. You do not wish to follow them now?'

'I'd like to,' said Ellis, 'but we'd better get the bodies back to town. The other miners must be told exactly who and what they are up against. Besides, there isn't time right now. We can start again in the morning. Have you decided how many of them there are?'

'Six horses,' said Joe. 'And one of the men has large feet and badly worn boots as before. I do not know if that tells you much but it tells me that this man has much pain when he walks. He twists his foot.'

'I don't know how you can tell,' said Ellis, 'but I'll take your word for it.'

★ ★ ★

The arrival of Ellis, Apache Joe and the two bodies caused a great stir in Mud City and it was not long before seemingly every prospector in the area was outside the saloon demanding to know exactly what Ellis was going to do about it.

'I'm doing my best,' said Ellis. 'Apache Joe seems to know which way they went and that there are six of them.'

'It looks like your best just ain't good enough,' called one of the prospectors. 'You're a marshal, it's your job to catch 'em.'

'I'm not arguing with that,' said Ellis, 'and catch them I will.'

'Fine words, Marshal,' the man called again. 'That's all they are though. How many more are goin' to be murdered before you do?'

'There's six of them, remember,' said Ellis. 'If they are going to be caught I'm going to need help.'

'Word is that they murdered another marshal and five deputies,' called another man. 'If they couldn't catch 'em what use will we be?'

'And what chance do I have on my own?' countered Ellis. 'These men are after gold, as much as they can get their hands on. Just remember that it's your gold.'

'It's up to you to protect us and our gold,' the man called again.

'I'm not here to protect your gold,' said Ellis. 'I'm here to try and stop these men killing anyone else and to try and get them back into prison where they belong. If you want to make sure they don't get their hands on everything you've worked hard for, you'd better get together and make sure they can't.'

'There won't be no need to send 'em back to prison, Marshal,' called another. 'If we get our hands on 'em there won't be nothin' left of 'em to send except a few pieces.'

'That'd be lynching,' said Ellis. 'Lynching is against the law.'

'Lynchin', Marshal?' the man said. 'We don't call it lynchin', out here we call it justice.'

'There'll be nothing like that as long as I'm around,' asserted Ellis.

'There's more'n three hundred of us, Marshal,' said another man. 'There's only one of you. How the hell do you reckon to stop us?'

'With these, if I have to,' replied Ellis, raising his rifle and tapping the gun at his side.

'I don't think so,' said Vince Parkes who, until that moment had remained silent. 'They have a point, Mr Stack. They have a right to expect justice. You might not agree with what form that justice takes, but I don't think that even you would deliberately kill a man who was demanding justice. Remember, I am a judge and since the murders have taken place in my area of jurisdiction, it is up to me what happens to these outlaws if and when they are caught.'

'Then it is also up to you to see that there is no lynch law,' said Ellis.

'I can assure you that they will receive a fair trial,' said Parkes. 'As far as I'm concerned it is your duty to bring them before my court. After that, their fate is my concern.'

Ellis chose not to argue the point. He was, reluctantly, forced to admit that

Vincent Parkes was technically correct even if he knew precisely what the outcome would be.

'OK, OK,' said Ellis. 'In the meantime I suggest that you all gather what gold you have and arrange for it all to be kept in one place. It seems to me that at least one of the outlaws must have some experience of just where prospectors hide their gold. I'm quite sure that the judge will be willing to keep it in his safe. You can mark your names on each pouch and it will be returned to you when you decide to leave.'

'That's fine by me,' said Parkes.

The men gathered in small groups and spent some time discussing the idea. Eventually, all except a few of them agreed to the proposal. The few who did not agree stated that they had decided they were quitting while they still had a chance.

'Cagney!' Amos Hutchinson suddenly called out. 'Cagney ain't here. Did you check on his claim?'

'There didn't seem much point,' said Ellis. 'The tracks led away from where he works.'

'But you never thought to check where the tracks came from.' said Hutchinson. 'They could've got to him first.'

'I'm on my way!' said Ellis. 'I should've thought of it before. Are you coming Joe?' He called to Apache Joe.

Ellis and Apache Joe raced out of Mud City and did not slow down until they had reached McFee's Basin. Once in the basin speed was impossible as they picked their way between rocks and boulders. Apache Joe apparently knew where Cagney's claim was.

Neither man was at all surprised when they discovered the body of the prospector.

★ ★ ★

'That does it, Mr Stack,' said Vince Parkes. 'If these men are caught there's no way I shall ever be able to hand them over to you. The miners will demand a hanging straight away and I for one don't intend to stand in their way.'

'Right now, Judge,' said Ellis, 'Exactly who is responsible for what is of no importance. The most important thing is to find these men before they kill anyone else.'

'And steal their gold,' added Parkes.

'I don't give a shit about the gold,' snapped Ellis. 'Five men in one day. Can you get everyone together? I'm going to need help and this ought to make them think twice.'

'It has,' said the judge. 'At least ten more have decided to get out while they can and a whole lot of the others are seriously thinking about it. Most have decided to hang on to their gold for a while yet while they consider what to do. That idea of yours was a good one but this sort of changes things. Mind you, I can't say that I'm too sorry. If word got to those outlaws that I had that much gold in my place they might just have a go at trying to relieve me of it.'

'Unless we catch these men there's a good chance that there won't be any gold left to put in that safe of yours,' said Ellis. 'See if you can get everybody together.'

It did not take long for all the miners to gather but they did not seem in any mood to compromise. Ellis's attempts to explain the law were met with jeers and he could see that he was wasting his time.

'The marshal is right,' said Parkes. 'You need to band together to stop these men. There's no knowing where they will strike next.'

'Form a posse, you mean,' called one. 'Marshal, all most of us have is shotguns or old muzzle-loaders an' they've got decent handguns an' rifles. We wouldn't stand a chance, no matter how many of us there are. I'll wager that there aren't more'n three or four decent guns or rifles in the territory an' those that do have 'em don't have that

119

much in the way of ammunition.'

'It's late now, too late to follow them,' said Ellis. 'Think about it. I'll be out here at first light waiting for volunteers. In the meantime I suggest that you all remain here where you will be fairly safe. They might attack anyone on their own but I don't think they'll try anything if you are all together.'

The men dispersed, talking amongst themselves, and Ellis was not very hopeful of finding any volunteers at all. He also learned that while he had been up at McFee's Basin the second time, several had packed up their belongings and were making their way out of Mud City.

'I have been thinking,' said Apache Joe as they watched the men disperse. 'I will help you.'

'Thanks, Joe,' said Ellis. 'I suppose two of us could be called a posse.'

'Do not blame them,' said Joe. 'They are right, they do not have the weapons with which to fight. They are not used to fighting unless it is with a knife.

There is one thing. I am bothered about the way we found those men and other things I have seen. Something is not right, I feel it in my bones. I am going back to Cagney's claim to take another look.'

'What for?' asked Ellis. 'You said yourself that there were six of them, all riding horses. We know that there are six outlaws and that they did head this way. Even I could see that their tracks headed south from Reese Pass.'

'That is true,' said Joe, 'but there is something else. I cannot say what it is but I must check. It could be that I am wasting my time, but it is mine to waste. For my own peace of mind I must find out.'

'OK, Joe,' said Ellis. 'It looks like I'm going to need all the help I can get. Let me know what you discover. In the meantime I'll try an' talk some sense into the miners. If I talk to them on their own they might come round to seeing some sense. All I can do is try.'

Apache Joe rode out of town and

Ellis approached various small groups of prospectors. He quickly discovered that even this more personal approach was not very successful.

Apache Joe arrived at Cagney's claim and immediately started to look about for signs that Mitchel Saunders and his men had been there. It did not take him too long to reach a conclusion.

★   ★   ★

'Are you quite certain, Joe?' asked Ellis when the Indian told him what he had found. 'The implication of what you are saying is that Cagney was *not* killed by Mitchel Saunders.'

'I am certain that the outlaws were never out at Cagney's claim,' said Joe. 'I checked the area all around and found no signs that horses had ever been there. I am also quite certain that the man with big feet and worn boots is not one of them. Although there had been no horses or other men who might have been the outlaws there, I did find imprints of the man with big feet.'

'Then what you are saying is that one or more of the prospectors murdered Cagney,' said Ellis.

'That is what it looks like to me,' said Joe. 'Come with me, there is something else I must show you.' He led Ellis outside to a piece of damp ground just outside the saloon. 'See, it is plain. A man with large feet and well-worn boots.'

'Sure, I see it,' conceded Ellis. 'But that could apply to any one of about three hundred men. I don't suppose worn boots are that unusual in a place like this. There's nowhere a man can buy new boots.'

'That is true,' admitted Joe. 'Perhaps it is nothing. Perhaps it has been too long since I last tracked a man. Perhaps I am getting old.'

'No, Joe, I don't think you are getting old. It's just that it doesn't make much sense, that's all.'

'Did you find out who has good guns?' asked Joe. 'Cagney was shot with a modern gun, not a shotgun or muzzle-loader, as were the others.'

'But we *do* know that Mitchel Saunders and his men *were* at the other two claims,' said Ellis.

'Yes, Marshal,' said Joe. 'The signs were very clear. They *were* there, but there is no doubt in my mind that they were not at Cagney's.'

'OK, Joe,' sighed Ellis. 'All I can do is take your word for it. Assuming that you are right, which I have no doubt you are, this means that somebody else murdered Cagney. That leaves about three hundred possible suspects. Have you any ideas?'

'Somebody who knew that Cagney had hit a rich supply of gold,' said Joe. 'I will ask if anyone knew if he had found a lot of gold lately.'

'Be careful, Joe,' advised Ellis. 'If anyone thinks that you are getting too close they won't hesitate to kill you as well and try to make it look like Mitchel Saunders did it, especially if they think you are working for me.'

'I will tell them that I too am leaving,' said Joe. 'Perhaps I will also say that I have a lot of gold with me.'

'I don't like it, Joe,' said Ellis. 'I don't like it at all. I had hoped that this would be nothing more than tracking down Mitchel Saunders. I hate it when complications like this happen. I suppose I had better tell Parkes.'

'Is that wise, Marshal?' asked Joe. 'Did you not say that there were about three hundred suspects and is not Mr Parkes one of that three hundred?'

'He is, I suppose,' conceded Ellis. 'But then so are you.'

'Yes, Marshal,' agreed Apache Joe. 'So am I.'

6

If Ellis had expected a quiet night in Mud City, he certainly did not get it. The room he had been given was at the front of the building and took the full brunt of noise both from the muddy street and the saloon below. He estimated that it was at least two o'clock in the morning before the doors of the saloon were finally closed. Even then there seemed to have been a drunken brawl taking place directly under his window.

On getting out of bed less than four hours later, a glance out of the window showed that some prospectors had packed and left during the night. He later learned that the majority of those who had left were those whose claims had proved unproductive and that most had only been hanging on in hope of better things. The happenings of the previous day had changed their minds.

Breakfast consisted of flapjacks and what was claimed to be syrup but Ellis had doubts about the exact ingredients of which each was made. The flapjacks had a distinctly gritty taste — sand or fine grit in flour to make it go further was a common practice — and the syrup was rather bitter and defied any attempt to suggest exactly from what it was made. The coffee was also another acquired taste and Ellis knew that in many remote parts it was nothing other than dried, boiled grass. However, he did manage to force it down. He discovered that a little of the syrup in the coffee helped the flavour of both.

He took the opportunity to question a couple of the girls who had risen early. Apparently it was unusual for anyone except the cook to be up much before ten o'clock. There was certainly no sign of Vince Parkes.

According to the girls, all of the murdered prospectors had apparently struck it rich during the previous two weeks and it seemed common knowledge that they each had a large amount of gold hidden somewhere on their claims.

Although three of the four claims in McFee's Basin had hit good supplies of gold, that belonging to Jimmy Grover and Amos Hutchinson had yielded very little. Amos Hutchinson was, apparently, very annoyed since he had previously owned the claim worked by Sam Benthall and Josh Brown. It seemed that he had lost it in a card game.

At the first real gold-strike on the lost claim, he had openly accused Benthall and Brown of cheating him at cards. The friction had almost ended in a fight. Judge Parkes had been called in to adjudicate and had apparently ruled in favour of Benthall and Brown keeping the claim.

After he had eaten, Ellis took up position outside the saloon, as he had said he would, and waited for volunteers to arrive to form a posse. In one hour his only volunteer appeared to be a small, mangy dog which settled at his feet.

Apache Joe appeared and both sat for some time on the narrow boardwalk watching the citizens of Mud City as they went about their business. Apart from a few curt nods, their existence seemed to go completely unnoticed and it was plain that there were not going to be any volunteers.

'I think we've got our posse,' said Ellis, sarcastically. 'You, me and the dog.'

'And I do not think the dog has a gun,' said Joe, with a broad grin. 'What are your plans for today, Marshal?'

'We ride out to Benthall and Brown's place and follow the tracks,' said Ellis. 'I know you think that somebody else might be responsible for those murders, particularly Cagney's, but finding those outlaws is still my main priority. Have you had any thoughts on who might have killed Cagney?'

'I have thought about it,' said Joe,

'and the more I think about it the more I am convinced that it must be Jimmy Grover and Amos Hutchinson.'

'Yes, I must admit that I also think that,' said Ellis. 'Come on, you can tell me why you think so as we ride.'

They rode slowly out of town, passing various prospectors who appeared to be in the process of vacating their claims.

'These murders certainly seem to have rattled them,' observed Ellis. 'Where will they go?'

'Most are going to Reese Pass,' said Joe. 'I have heard that a few are going down to Jackson where gold was discovered a couple of years ago. They say that Jackson is worked out, but prospectors always live in the hope that they will discover a rich claim. That is what keeps them going.'

'Including you?' asked Ellis.

'Yes, including me,' said Joe. 'My problem is keeping what I do find. I also have a problem in staking a claim. Indians are not welcome in most places. Mud City is the first place I have been where nobody seemed to mind.'

'I must admit that I didn't see any Indians in Reese Pass,' said Ellis. 'Are there many of you?'

'Not many,' said Joe. 'Most of my kind do not look upon gold in the same way as the white man.'

'OK, so what makes you think that it was Grover and Hutchinson who murdered Cagney?'

'After I left you last night,' said Joe, 'I saw Hutchinson walking down the street. I noticed that when he walked he twisted his left foot and I also saw that he has very large feet. I followed him and looked at the marks left in the mud and I am quite certain that they are the same as the footprints we found at McFee's Basin.'

'Unfortunately, worn boots alone would not be proof,' said Ellis. 'I dare say that there are a good many others whose boots are in the same condition, just as I am sure that there are others with feet the same size as Amos Hutchinson.' Ellis raised his leg from his stirrup and nodded. 'My feet are pretty big.'

'This I know,' said Joe. 'It is just that I feel in my bones that he is the man.'

'What about Jimmy Grover?' asked Ellis.

'There are no signs to link him with the murder,' admitted Joe. 'I do not think that Hutchinson would act on his own though. You would have more proof if they were found to have a lot of gold.'

'Even that wouldn't prove a thing,' said Ellis. 'As far as I know there's no way of proving exactly where any gold came from no matter how much a man had. It could easily be argued that they kept the amount secret precisely because they feared someone might steal it. Gold is gold as far as I'm concerned and I think the law would have much the same view. Apart from the imprints of worn boots and large feet, did you find signs of anyone else being there?'

'It is difficult to say,' said Joe. 'Jimmy

Grover's feet are not large, probably the same size as most men's. There were signs of another man, but I cannot say that they were not made by Cagney himself. Why do you think that they murdered Cagney?'

'Like you,' said Ellis, 'it's just a feeling. I know McFee's Basin is about two miles across, but gunfire in a place like that would easily be heard over that distance. The shape is ideal for creating echoes. They claim that they didn't hear a thing but I can't believe that.'

'I know both of them,' said Joe. 'They are not clever men. I do not think that either of them can read or write.'

'That doesn't make them fools though,' said Ellis. 'Can you read and write?'

'I was taught by missionaries when I was a child,' said Joe. 'I know that not being able to do such things does not make a man a fool, but both of them do not seem to have much in their heads.'

'What's your point, Joe?' asked Ellis.

'It is simple,' said Joe. 'If it had been

me or some other men, I would have said that I had heard shooting. That way they would have pointed suspicion directly at this Mitchel Saunders. Because they are simple and it was them who did the shooting, they did not want to attract attention to themselves.'

'Then why bring the bodies of Smith and Palmer into town?' prompted Ellis.

'That too is easy to explain,' said Joe. 'Simple they might be, but not that simple. They knew that the claim belonging to Smith and Palmer was easily seen from the trail and they realized that it would have looked strange if they had rode past and not seen the bodies.'

'Or it could just be that Saunders and his men *were* there and *did* murder Smith and Palmer,' said Ellis. 'Perhaps it was finding them which gave Hutchinson and Grover the idea of murdering Cagney.'

'I am surprised at you, Marshal,' said Joe, with a broad smile. 'Hutchinson and Grover were in Mud City all day. They did not go back to McFee's Basin. The murder of Cagney took place *before* they brought the bodies back to town.'

'Then why didn't they bring the body of Cagney as well?'

'Because they are simple men and it did not occur to them,' said Joe. 'The body of Cagney might have lain there for days before being discovered. The same thing goes for Benthall and Brown. The same boot-mark was at all three places but Saunders was only at two of them.'

'So you're saying that either Hutchinson or Grover or both murdered all five men?' said Ellis.

'That is what I am saying, Marshal,' said Joe. 'If you require proof, that is something I cannot provide other than the evidence of my own eyes and the feelings within my bones.'

'All five were killed with modern guns,' said Ellis. 'There were too many bullets in each body for a muzzle-loader to have been used. It would have taken too long to reload even if they both had muzzle-loaders. Do Hutchinson and Grover have a modern gun? They certainly didn't bring one into town with them.'

'Neither did I,' said Joe.

They reached McFee's Basin and the first thing Ellis decided to do was to take another look at where Cagney had been found. Joe pointed out the marks made by the worn boot and large feet and also the fact that there was no sign of horses or a group of other men having been there. The only signs of any animals were those made, according to Joe, by a mule or mules. Ellis was forced to admit that had he been on his own he would not have noticed any of those things and certainly would not be able to tell the difference between horse and mule tracks.

Now completely satisfied that he was faced with a murder or even murders committed by Amos Hutchinson and Jimmy Groves or, just possibly, by one of the other prospectors, Ellis turned his attention to looking for Mitchel Saunders.

They picked up the tracks left by the outlaws at the claim worked by Sam Benthall and Josh Brown. Apache Joe pointed out the marks of the man with big feet and worn boots and Ellis was forced to admit that they looked exactly the same as those at Cagney's workings.

'You know, Joe,' said Ellis, 'I think you're right about them being responsible for all the murders. It seems obvious that Hutchinson at least has been to all three places. If he had found them all dead, there would have been no need to hide the fact. In a way, his mistake was taking Smith's and Palmer's bodies into town and claiming it was Mitchel Saunders.'

'Did he know about Saunders before you told him?' asked Joe. 'I think so, it seems that most folk did. Didn't you?'

'There was a rumour, that is all,' said Joe.

'Rumour is enough in most cases,' said Ellis.

They followed the tracks made by Mitchel Saunders and his men out of the basin and then through a narrow gap between two hills. Half an hour later they came across the remains of a fire and evidence of a goat having been slaughtered and cooked. Joe felt the ashes and the remains of the goat and announced that both were about two days old.

'These are the same tracks we found at the other two claims,' said Joe. 'From here they lead up through that small pass between the mountains. Do we follow?'

'We follow,' said Ellis. 'First we find the outlaws.'

'And when we find them?' asked Joe.

'That's something I'll have to think about,' said Ellis. 'I'd like to talk to them and find out if those prospectors *were* dead before they arrived. Where does that pass lead to?'

'That I do not know,' said Joe. 'I feel

that it will eventually lead into Big Smokey Valley.'

'Well, there's one sure way to find out,' said Ellis. 'Let's go.'

They had followed the tracks for another four hours when Joe suddenly stopped and pointed down into a narrow valley.

'They are down there,' he said. 'See, there are horses alongside that river. It looks to me like they have settled there for a while; the horses do not carry saddles.' Ellis took out his spyglass and surveyed the valley. Eventually he grunted and handed the spyglass to Joe.

'They're among that clump of trees,' said Ellis. 'About thirty yards away from the horses. Can we get close without being seen?'

'It will not be easy,' said Joe. 'The hardest part will be getting down into the valley. It is open ground for about a mile and it only needs one of them to look that way to see us. If we can get down without being seen we have a better chance.'

'Then we can either take the chance or wait for them to move on,' said Ellis. As they watched, one of the men appeared and saddled a horse. There appeared to be a conversation taking place and some pointing. Eventually the man rode off and seemed to be heading south. It was impossible to tell if the man was one of the original escapees or not.

'How far away do you think Mud City is from here?' asked Ellis.

'I think that we have come around in a circle,' said Joe. 'That is how it seems to me. From here I think that Mud City can only be about five or six miles.'

'Then I think that he has been sent to Mud City,' said Ellis. 'If we are right and those prospectors were dead when they found them, they must want to know what is going on. I think that he has been sent to find out.'

'You might be right,' said Joe. 'What do we do now?'

'Well, I think it's too risky to try and get down there,' said Ellis. 'I suggest we get back to Mud City and find out from him what they know. Do we have to go all the way round again?'

'I think not,' said Joe. 'See that mountain,' he pointed at a tall peak. 'I think that is the big mountain behind Mud City. From here it is no more than six miles, but I do not know how easy it will be.'

'Then let's find out,' said Ellis. 'At least we know Mitchel Saunders is close by. We can deal with him later.'

The way back to Mud City, although involving a lot of climbing and twisting and turning, was not too difficult even if slower than it might have been. It took them almost two hours to reach the town. The first thing Ellis did was to remove his badge so as not to alert the outlaw — if he had arrived — as to who he was.

Since horses were a comparatively rare sight — mules being the usual mode of transport — it was easy to pick out where any strangers might be. In this case there was a solitary horse tethered outside the saloon. Judging by the equipment, or rather the lack of equipment, associated with prospectors, Ellis knew that this was the horse they had seen earlier.

They went into the saloon where Joe, without being asked or told, took up a position by the door. Ellis approached the bar and the only man who appeared out of place, who was leaning on the counter.

'Afternoon,' grunted Ellis as he leaned on the counter alongside the man. He flashed a quick warning look at the bartender who appeared to take the hint, served Ellis with a beer and went to the far end of the counter.

'Afternoon,' grunted the man in reply.

'Stranger here, ain't you?' said Ellis. 'We don't get many strangers in Mud City.'

'Can't say as I'm surprised,' said the man. 'Who the hell would want to come to a dump like this?'

'Folk like you, apparently,' said Ellis.

'You don't look like a prospector. What brings you here?'

'Just passin' through,' said the man. 'It looks like I'm just in time before the town closes. I seen a hell of a lot of folk leavin'.'

'Too many prospectors, not enough gold,' said Ellis. 'That isn't the real reason though; most folk are running in fear of their lives.'

'Runnin' from what or who?' asked the man.

'A bunch of outlaws,' said Ellis. 'They broke out of prison at Winnemucca and word has it that they've killed about eight people before they reached here and now they're killing the miners and stealing their gold.'

'Killing the miners?' queried the man.

The look on the man's face told Ellis all he wanted to know. It seemed that he was genuinely surprised. The look was a fleeting one and was quickly replaced by a knowing smile.

'Five miners have been murdered by

these men at a place called McFee's basin about five miles out of town,' said Ellis. 'You don't happen to have seen six men who might be outlaws on your travels do you?'

'Nope,' replied the man. 'Why so interested?'

'It's my job,' said Ellis, taking his badge out of his pocket and showing it. 'US Marshal Ellis Stack.'

'Then the miners don't have nothin' to worry about,' said the man, plainly uneasy. 'What's a marshal doin' in a dump like this?'

'Looking for the outlaws,' said Ellis. 'Maybe you've heard of them. There's Mitchel Saunders, he apparently heads the bunch, Lefty Swann, James Coburn and a mad man named Seamus Docherty. I hear he's really wild. They're the ones who escaped from prison in Winnemucca. They were joined by three others, but I know that one of them, Joe Daniels, decided he'd had enough and got out. The other two are Luke Franks and Josh Wellings. I don't know much about them except their names. Which one are you, Franks or Wellings?'

'What you talkin' about?' said the man, standing up straight but refusing to look Ellis in the eye.

'You heard me,' said Ellis. 'What's your name, Franks or Wellings?'

'That's a dangerous accusation, Marshal,' grated the man. 'I'm just a stranger passin' through.'

The man straightened up a little more and allowed his hand to slip towards his gun.

'Think you can take me?' said Ellis, also straightening up. 'There's a gun aimed at your back right now.'

The man looked round to see Apache Joe, rifle in hand and aimed at him, about five feet away. He cursed and raised his hand away from his gun.

'The name's Smith,' he said. 'Conrad Smith. I don't know what you're talkin' about, Marshal.'

'Smith!' said Ellis with a dry laugh. 'It seems to me there's an awful lot of

Smiths about these days.'

'It's a common enough name,' said the man. 'I can't help the name I was born with can I?'

'I guess not,' said Ellis, 'but I don't believe you. Me and Joe were up in the mountains earlier and we saw a man who looked exactly like you leave the other five. Between you, you have committed thirteen murders in less than a week. That's a lot of killings even by Seamus Docherty's standards. So far you've murdered a farmer and his wife, a US Marshal called Tom Burns, five of his deputies and now five prospectors. You have also stolen their gold.'

'I don't know what you're talkin' about,' grated the man. 'I came into town by myself. I've been on the road from Eureka for more'n a week so I don't know a thing about no killings.'

'I don't think so,' said Ellis. 'Now, what do I call you, Luke Franks or Josh Wellings?'

'You call me Conrad Smith,' insisted the man.

'OK, Mr Conrad Smith,' said Ellis. 'It really doesn't matter to me what you choose to call yourself. I am arresting you for the murder of five prospectors if nothing else. The man who owns this saloon also happens to be a judge and since the murders of the prospectors took place in his jurisdiction I have to hand you over to him. Don't worry, you'll get a fair trial before they hang you. Probably the trial will take place in the morning and the hanging tomorrow afternoon.'

'Now look here, Marshal,' croaked the man. 'That don't sound like no fair trial to me. My name's Smith I tell you an' I don't know a damned thing about no outlaws or the murders of no prospectors.'

'Then you have nothing to worry about, do you?' said Ellis. 'I'm sure Judge Parkes will be very fair. In the meantime you are under arrest on suspicion if nothing else. Come on, I need to find a safe place to keep you. If you try to escape I don't think you'll get very far and I can't say what'll happen to you. Lynching is the usual way of justice out here.'

The man looked about and already there was quite a sizeable crowd gathering in the bar, most of them muttering about a hanging. The man licked his lips and was sweating profusely.

'You wouldn't dare let them lynch me,' he croaked. 'You're a US marshal, lynchin' is against the law.'

'So is murder,' said Ellis.

'OK, OK,' the man said hoarsely. 'I admit it, I am with Saunders, I didn't kill nobody though. The name's Josh Wellings. I'm a nobody, just a small time outlaw what got mixed up with somethin' he shouldn't't've.'

'That's better,' said Ellis. 'There's an office over there.' He nodded at the office door. 'We can talk in there. Joe, stand guard on the door, I don't want nobody getting the idea of taking the law into their own hands.'

Ellis took the gun from Wellings and

he was ushered into the office. Almost immediately almost all those present were making demands for a hanging. Vince Parkes also followed Ellis into the office, insisting that, as a judge, he was entitled.

'OK, Mr Parkes,' agreed Ellis, 'but I'll do the talking. He isn't charged with anything yet.'

Ellis sat in the only chair behind the desk and stared at Wellings for a few moments. He placed his gun on the desk, making a point of having the barrel facing towards Wellings.

'You can't let them hang me,' croaked Wellings. 'That'd be lynching an' it's against the law.'

'I'm just one man,' said Ellis. 'I wouldn't be able to stop them. Now, I do know that you are responsible for the murders of the farmer and his wife and Marshal Burns and his deputies . . .'

'It was Docherty what killed the farmer and his wife,' croaked Wellings. 'You're right about him, he's completely mad. He kills just for the hell of it.'

'And Marshal Tom Burns?' prompted Ellis.

'OK, I was there,' admitted Wellings. 'I didn't kill none of 'em though, I made sure of that. Killing a lawman is as good as signin' your own death warrant, I know that.'

'I have only your word for that,' said Ellis. 'Now, what about the murders of the prospectors?'

'We didn't kill any of 'em,' said Wellings, laughing nervously. 'Sure, we went to two claims lookin' for gold but we didn't find any. You can believe this or not, but it's true, them miners was already dead when we went there. I only saw four of 'em though, but I suppose there could've been five.'

'Already dead?' asked Vince Parkes. 'You can't expect us to believe that. The other miner was — '

'I'll do the questioning, Mr Parkes,' interrupted Ellis. 'So, Mr Wellings, you went to two claims and they were already dead. Can you prove that?'

'How the hell do you expect me to do

that?' said Wellings. 'I reckon you've decided on a lynchin' already an' the truth don't matter no more.'

'The truth *does* matter, Mr Wellings, to me at least.' said Ellis. 'Is there anywhere this man can be held safely, Mr Parkes?'

'There's a shed at the back,' said Parkes. 'He can be tied up in there. You'll have to post a guard though.'

'Apache Joe can look after him,' said Ellis.

7

Josh Wellings was securely tied up in the shed and Apache Joe took up position outside the door. Ellis returned to the bar and found the miners in a decidedly nasty mood.

'They're demanding a hanging,' said Vince Parkes. 'I don't know if I'll be able to stop them.'

'Let's talk in your office,' said Ellis. 'There's a couple of things I think you ought to know.'

The two men went into the office, leaving the door slightly ajar so that Ellis could make sure that nobody was listening. He seated himself at the desk, leaving the judge to stand.

'I'm waiting, Marshal,' said Parkes. 'This had better be good because the mood they're in means that they won't be satisfied until this Wellings is swinging on the end of a rope.'

'How about if I tell you that Mitchel Saunders and his men did not murder those miners?' said Ellis.

'You might as well tell me that I can fly,' said Parkes. 'There's a bunch of known outlaws — killers — out there and on his own admission Wellings was one of them. It stands to reason that they *must* be the killers.'

'Well I think I can safely say that they did not murder those miners,' said Ellis. He went on to explain exactly what he and Apache Joe had discovered. He did not mention who he thought was responsible.

'Pure conjecture, Marshal,' said Parkes. 'You can't prove a damned thing.'

'Nor is there any proof that Saunders did it,' said Ellis.

'Good God, Marshal!' exclaimed Parkes. 'Six outlaws, all known killers. You have admitted as much yourself. You know they murdered the farmer and his wife. You know that they killed Marshal Burns and his deputies. They turn up in Mud City and five more men are killed. What more proof do you want?'

'OK,' said Ellis. 'It certainly looks bad for Saunders and his men. That is precisely what the real killers want you to believe. So you hang Wellings and that may well be what he deserves, but not for these murders. In hanging him you allow the real murderers of the prospectors to go free. Is that what you want?'

'I don't give a damn what happens to the outlaws,' snapped Parkes.

'Frankly, neither do I,' said Ellis. 'I aim to see that they answer for what they have done, but I also intend to see that the real killers of the prospectors are also brought to justice. That's my job and, as a judge, it ought to be yours. Just remember that I could quite easily have you taken off the list of judges. I've done it before and I have no doubt that I will do so again.'

Vince Parkes sat on the edge of the desk and remained silent for a while, obviously thinking.

'You seem pretty certain about it,' Parkes said eventually.

'I am,' said Ellis. 'I agree that Mitchel Saunders and his men must be brought to justice to answer for what they've done and I intend to see that they are. In the meantime it's up to you and me to make sure that there are no lynchings.'

'OK, Mr Stack,' said Parkes. 'So far though you haven't said who you think is responsible. If you want me to co-operate I think you owe me that much at least.'

'I was coming to that. I believe that Jimmy Grover and Amos Hutchinson did it,' said Ellis.

'Grover and Hutchinson!' exclaimed Parkes. 'It was them who found Smith and Palmer and brought their bodies into town. They wouldn't do a damned fool thing like that if they were guilty.'

'They thought they had the perfect alibi,' said Ellis. 'A bunch of known killers on the loose in the area. What could be better? I think it is also common knowledge that the outlaws were after gold. A more perfect set of circumstances could never have arisen.'

The judge lapsed into silence again and thought deeply. Eventually he stood up and paced the room for a while.

'If what you say about the footprint is correct in that it was found at all three claims and that Saunders and his men had only been at two of them, then I agree that Grover and Hutchinson have some questions to answer,' he said eventually. 'I also happen to know that they both have a couple of old Newbury revolvers as well as a muzzle-loading rifle and a shotgun each. However, I am sure that you are aware that the presence of a footprint alone is not sufficient proof. There could be any number of men with big feet and worn boots, probably even one of the outlaws.'

'I don't think so,' said Ellis. 'Joe and me found where they'd made camp and there were plenty of footprints about but none of them matched the one found at the workings. It would seem to me that you are prepared to let this man hang on far less evidence than a footprint. You can't have it both ways.'

'It looks like you've made up your mind,' said Parkes. 'OK, Marshal, I must admit that what you say sounds very plausible. I think I can persuade them out there not to try anything at the moment, but I don't know for how long. Once they get it into their heads that someone is guilty it's a hell of a job to shift them. Anyhow, if you want to prove that it was Grover and Hutchinson who did it you'd better be quick about it. I heard last night that they've decided to leave Mud City, but I don't think they've gone yet.'

'It shouldn't be too difficult,' said Ellis. 'I'll search them before they go and if I find a large amount of gold I think that will be proof enough. In the meantime it's up to you to make sure the others don't get Wellings from the shed and hang him.'

'And what about Saunders and his men?' asked Parkes. 'They're still out there and we know they are not afraid to kill. They have to be caught.'

'And catch them I will, Mr Parkes,' said Ellis. 'Just remember this though. Those men are wanted by the state for murders committed elsewhere and as such are outside your area of jurisdiction. I shall take them back to be tried by a judge who does have the authority to try them for what they've done. For the moment, though, I don't think that the others should be told about Grover and Hutchinson.'

'If I'm to keep them from Wellings, they have to be told something,' said Parkes.

'I don't care what you tell them,' said Ellis. 'Just make sure, that's all.'

'If you think I'm going to stand in their way if they break into the shed then you've got another think coming,' said Parkes. 'They won't think twice about killing Apache Joe either. Killing an Indian in this state isn't counted as murder, not like killing a white man. The most any man can get for killing an Indian is a one-hundred-dollar fine and most don't even get to court. You ought to know that.'

'I am well aware of that fact, Mr Parkes,' said Ellis. 'It is something I have never agreed with but, as you say, that is the law. The difference is I've made Joe a deputy marshal an' killing a deputy marshal is a hanging offence, Indian or not. You make sure they know that.'

'OK, Mr Stack,' said Parkes with a resigned sigh. 'It looks like you've thought of everything. I'll see what I can do.'

Ellis went back to the shed and told Joe that he was now a deputy marshal and as such he would be paid for his services.

'Thanks for that,' said Joe. 'I ain't never heard of an Indian deputy marshal before. I know there are Indian police in some parts and on the reservations, but that's not quite the same thing. Do I get a badge?'

'Sorry, I don't carry badges around with me,' said Ellis with a broad smile. 'Everybody in Mud City will know by now though, so you won't have any trouble.'

'They won't like it,' said Joe.

'Does that bother you?' asked Ellis.

'No, sir, it does not,' said Joe, laughing. 'Imagine that, me, Jottie Washakie, Apache Joe, a deputy US marshal.'

'I don't think there'll be any trouble tonight,' said Ellis, 'but I don't like the idea of leaving Wellings with Vince Parkes. I'm going to need you to help me so I can't afford to leave you here to stand guard over him.'

'I have been thinking about that,' said Joe 'I have an idea . . . '

★　★　★

Vince Parkes was up very early the following morning and even woke Ellis. He was plainly very worried.

'I told them about Apache Joe being

made a deputy,' he said to Ellis, 'Most of them said that they wouldn't pay no attention to an Indian even if he is a deputy marshal. They also said that they were coming to get Wellings this morning and that I was to hold a trial just to make it all legal.'

'Of course you said you wouldn't?' said Ellis.

'No, sir, I said I would,' replied Parkes. 'I've been thinking about what you said and I don't buy it. I'm sure it was Mitchel Saunders and his men and so is everybody else. I'm sorry Mr Stack, but out here justice is swift, it has to be, we don't have jails or prisons to hold folk like that. There was a meeting outside, it's a wonder you didn't notice. They made it plain they were going to have a hanging even if I didn't hold a trial.'

'So you thought you'd better hold a trial just to cover yourself,' said Ellis. 'OK, I guess I can't stop you, I'm a marshal, not a judge. There is one thing though. I'll wager that Amos Hutchinson and Jimmy Grover did most of the talking.'

'They said their piece,' admitted Parkes.

'I thought they might,' said Ellis. 'There is just one thing going to stop you holding your trial though. Josh Wellings isn't in the shed. In fact he isn't even in town. I thought something like this might happen so I had him moved.'

'Moved him!' exclaimed Parkes. 'You had no right to do that.'

'I have every right,' said Ellis. 'Lynching is against the law, Judge, and what you propose is nothing more than a lynching. Under those circumstances I, as a US marshal, have a duty to protect the accused. I have merely exercised my duty.'

'I hope you realize that this is going to make things even worse,' complained Parkes. 'They'll find him and when they do there's nothing I'll be able to do to prevent them from hanging him.'

'They have to find him first,' said Ellis. 'Now, have you heard any more about Grover and Hutchinson leaving town?'

'They're almost packed up and ready to go,' said Parkes.

'Good, I'll go and search through their belongings,' said Ellis. 'I want you with me as a witness. If I don't find any large amounts of gold I'll admit defeat and you can have Wellings.'

'They claim that they don't have much,' said Parkes. 'Personally I don't think you'll find any more than might be expected. I'll hold you to your promise.'

'I always keep my word,' said Ellis. 'Just as I expect you to accept the fact that they are guilty if I do find a lot of gold.'

'It's a deal, Mr Stack,' promised Parkes.

They found Jimmy Grover and Amos Hutchinson in the process of loading one of their three mules. They both looked very uncomfortable when they saw Ellis and the judge approaching.

'Where's your new deputy?' asked

Hutchinson, with a weak laugh.

'He's around,' said Ellis. 'I see you are packing up and leaving. I would have thought you would want to stay around and see Wellings on the end of a rope. It was you who found Smith and Palmer, so you are witnesses.'

'Witnesses to what, Marshal?' asked Grover. 'Like you say, all we did was find 'em. We didn't see or hear anythin'. Anyhow, we ain't that bothered about seein' a man hang.'

'So you say,' said Ellis. 'I still find it very difficult to understand how you didn't hear anything but I suppose it's possible. So, you've decided to get out. That's your right of course and, as you say, you only found the bodies so you are not vital witnesses. Where are you going?'

'We figured on tryin' our luck down in Jackson,' said Hutchinson. 'Reese Pass ain't the place for us, there's too many up there.'

'You might strike it lucky,' said Ellis. 'From what I hear you certainly have not had much luck in Mud City.'

'We found a bit,' said Grover. 'Enough to get us by for a couple of weeks.' He glared at the judge. 'We would've hit it big if we hadn't been cheated out of our claim,' he said to the judge. 'We know Benthall an' Brown hit a big seam an' were goin' back East to retire. Now it looks like them outlaws have got it all.'

'That's what you'd like everybody to believe,' said Ellis.

'Meanin' what, Marshal?' grated Hutchinson.

'Meaning exactly that,' said Ellis.

'What you gettin' at?' demanded Grover. 'It sounds to me like you're accusin' us of somethin'.'

'I am not accusing anyone of anything,' said Ellis. 'I am investigating the murders of five of your fellow prospectors, that's all.'

'Then you've got one of the killers,' said Grover. 'The others are out there somewhere. Why ain't you out there lookin' for 'em instead of harassin' decent folk like us?'

'I'm simply trying to tie up a few loose ends, Mr Grover,' said Ellis.

'Loose ends!' snarled Hutchinson. 'Seems to me that you is the loose end round here.'

'Perhaps so,' said Ellis. 'Since you obviously have nothing to hide, I wonder if you would allow me to search your belongings?'

'You can go to hell, Marshal,' grated Hutchinson.

'That could be where I'll end up when I die,' said Ellis. 'In the meantime, I intend to search no matter what you say.'

'An' we say you ain't,' snarled Grover. Ellis suddenly found himself looking at two pistols. 'You ain't got no right, US Marshal or not,' continued Grover. 'We're leavin', Mr Stack, an' you ain't about to stop us.'

'Are you prepared to use those guns?' said Ellis. 'If you want to stop me you'd better be prepared to and to answer for the consequences.' Both men looked nervously at each other and lowered their guns slightly. 'Stand aside while I look,' continued Ellis.

'And the first one who tries anything will be shot,' said a voice. Apache Joe came from behind a tent, rifle aimed at the two prospectors.

'Indian bastard!' snarled Hutchinson. 'I should've known you'd be around somewhere. I thought I could smell somethin'.'

'I'll take those guns,' said Ellis reaching forward and taking them. 'They'll be given back to you if I don't find anything.'

'Like what?' demanded Grover.

'Like an unusual amount of gold,' said Ellis.

'OK, OK,' said Hutchinson. 'So we got a bit more'n we said we had. There ain't no law what says we have to tell anyone how much we've got. We figured it best not to tell anybody so's they think we wasn't worth robbin'.'

'How much more, Mr Hutchinson?'

asked Ellis. 'You can start by emptying your pockets.'

The two men glanced at Apache Joe, who waved his gun slightly and they proceeded to empty their pockets. By that time a large crowd had gathered but was strangely silent.

The contents of their pockets showed nothing out of the ordinary other than two leather pouches — one on each man — each containing gold. Ellis had to admit that the amount involved, although rather more than they had claimed, was insufficient to prove that it had been stolen.

'I've no idea how much gold is worth,' he said to the judge. 'What do you reckon?'

'Maybe a thousand dollars each,' said Parkes.

'Not bad, but hardly enough for a man to retire on,' said Ellis. 'Is that all?' he said to the men.

'That's all,' said Hutchinson. 'Can we go now?'

'Not yet,' said Ellis. 'I'll take a look

through this lot.'

Ellis started to search through the contents on the back of the pack mule despite protests from Grover and Hutchinson. Initially the search revealed absolutely nothing other than what might have been expected. Ellis even unrolled their tent but was still unable to find a thing. He looked at Vince Parkes who had a satisfied smirk on his face and then at Apache Joe. He shrugged as if admitting that he had been wrong.

'Under the blanket or under the saddles of the other mules,' suggested Joe.

There was a frame across the back of the pack mule with a blanket under it. Ellis told Jimmy Grover to remove both blanket and frame but there was nothing to be found. He then ordered the men to remove the saddles on the other mules.

'You're wastin' your time, Mr Stack,' complained Amos Hutchinson. 'We don't have what you're lookin' for, that's obvious, ain't it?'

'When I see what is or is not under those saddles,' insisted Ellis.

'Have it your way,' grumbled Jimmy Grover. 'You won't find nothin' though.'

'I'd rather check that for myself,' said Ellis. 'If I'm wrong, I apologize.'

Both men smirked and untied the saddles and removed them. Ellis stripped off the blanket underneath and, much to his dismay, found nothing.

'Told you so,' said Hutchinson, laughing. 'We told you, the men you want are out there somewhere.'

Ellis was about to admit that he had obviously been wrong when Apache Joe stepped forward and grabbed the saddle off Jimmy Grover.

'What the hell do you think you is doin', you Indian bastard?' hissed Grover, attempting to snatch the saddle back. 'You ain't got no right to take that saddle even if you is a deputy marshal. Mr Stack, get this animal off me before I kill him, deputy or no deputy.'

'Leave him, Joe,' said Ellis. 'It looks like I owe them and the judge an apology.'

'Apology accepted, Mr Stack,' said Hutchinson, grinning broadly.

'Not yet,' insisted Joe, this time succeeding in wrenching the saddle away from Jimmy Grover.

Despite an attempt by Grover to regain possession, Joe was able to turn the saddle over in the mud.

'What the hell do you think you is playin' at?' demanded Grover.

'I am not playing,' said Joe.

There was nothing to be seen under the saddle but that did not deter Apache Joe who took out a knife and, despite protests from the two prospectors and Judge Vince Parkes, cut at some stitching on the lining underneath. Almost immediately he pulled out a leather pouch. He cut at some more stitching and another pouch was revealed. He then grabbed the saddle from Amos Hutchinson and did the same to that. This time there were three leather pouches. Ellis and Judge Parkes loosened the ties and emptied some of the contents into the palms of their hands. All the prospectors gathered round immediately started shouting at once.

'Well,' said Ellis. 'I think that there is rather more gold here than there ought to be. How much do you think, Judge?'

'There must be something like twenty thousand dollars' worth at least,' replied the judge. 'Can you explain this?' he said to the two men.

'I don't think there's any need for them to explain anything,' said Ellis, holding up one of the pouches. 'There's a name on this. It says S BENTHALL. The only S Benthall I know is the Sam Benthall who was murdered.'

'This one has a name on it as well,' said Parkes. 'H CAGNEY. I never did know Cagney's first name. It looks like you two have got quite a bit of explaining to do.'

'OK, OK,' said Hutchinson. 'I admit it, we took the gold, but we didn't kill them. We only did what anybody else would've done.'

'Sure,' said Jimmy Grover. 'We found them dead an' we looked for their gold. Maybe we shouldn't've done but I defy any man here to say that he wouldn't've done the same. We figured that since they were dead the gold belonged to any man what found it.'

'I don't believe you,' said Ellis. 'Hutchinson, lift up your left boot.'

'Lift up my . . . What the hell for?' demanded Amos Hutchinson. 'Just lift up your boot,' ordered Ellis.

Grumbling and complaining loudly, Amos Hutchinson did as he was told. The boot was almost worn through and Ellis reminded Judge Parkes of what they had discovered at the claims.

'We just admitted we were there,' said Hutchinson. 'So, you found my footprint, that don't prove nothin'. It sure don't prove we murdered any of them.'

'It raises a lot of interesting questions though,' said Ellis. 'The fact that there was no sign of the outlaws having been anywhere near Cagney's place can only mean that you must've killed him.'

'And we say that he was dead when we found him,' said Jimmy Grover. 'Saunders must've made a good job of coverin' his tracks, that's all I can say.'

'Then why did he not try to cover his tracks at the other claims?' asked Ellis. 'You brought the bodies of Smith and Palmer into town because you knew that anyone using the trail would be bound to see them. You brought them in to cover yourselves. If the others were dead when you found them, why didn't you bring in their bodies too. At least you could have told the judge or me what you had found.'

'I guess we panicked,' said Jimmy Grover. 'Sure, we brought them two into town 'cos they could be seen, just like you said. We knew what everybody would think if it got round that we'd taken the gold, so we kept quiet.'

'I hear that stealing another man's gold is a hanging offence out here,' said Ellis. 'The fact that all the men were dead does not make it legal to take their gold. It should have been handed to Judge Parkes so that he could arrange for it to be sent to any relatives of the dead men. I think that you murdered those men and hoped that Saunders would be blamed. It almost worked too. I am arresting you for the murders of Smith, Palmer, Benthall, Brown and Cagney. I am also charging you with stealing gold.'

'And since the murders took place in Mud City they come under my jurisdiction,' said the judge. 'The trial will take place in one hour in the saloon.'

'Marshal!' wailed Amos Hutchinson. 'You can't hand us over to him. We've seen the way a court operates out here. We don't stand a chance. There'll be a farce of a trial an' then we'll be taken out an' hanged.'

'I can't say that I agree with the way trials are held,' said Ellis, 'but Judge Parkes is quite right, they did happen in his area of authority. I'm sorry, there's nothing I can do about it. I wonder how many times you have objected when other men have been accused of stealing gold or murder?'

'This is different!' cried Hutchinson. 'We didn't kill 'em.'

'It's always different,' said Ellis.

8

Although he had heard and had been told by Judge Parkes of justice being swift in the more remote parts, Ellis was not quite prepared for just how swift that justice was in reality. In less than an hour the saloon had been turned into a makeshift courtroom and Judge Parkes had sworn in a jury. There seemed little doubt in Ellis's mind that a verdict had been reached even before the jury had been sworn in. He overheard several of the jurors saying that it was a waste of time and that they ought to get on with the hanging.

'Your honour,' said Ellis when proceedings began. 'I can't help but feel that the speed with which this action is being taken is rather too hasty. I feel that it is unfair on the defendants and formally request an adjournment in order that they may prepare their case.'

'Marshal Stack,' intoned Judge Parkes in his most officious voice. 'I must remind you of your position. As a US marshal you have done everything expected of you — admirably I might add. You have pursued, rightly so, your duties in apprehending the murderers of five prospectors and the theft of their gold. I must admit that I did differ from you as to the likely perpetrators of these crimes and I admit that I was wrong. I must also remind you that it was you who arrested these men on evidence which you, yourself, gathered. That is the point at which your duties cease. From now on what happens to these men is a matter for the legally constituted court. You are not a lawyer, you are a United States Marshal. The crimes with which Amos Hutchinson and James Grover have been charged took place in my area of jurisdiction and it is my intention to administer justice according to the law as I am empowered so to do. It is part of the constitution of these great states that the administration of justice is founded on trial by a jury formed by the peers of these men. Whilst I note your submission, I can see no reason why the proceedings should be further delayed. Your objection is overruled. Bring on the accused and allow proceedings to commence according to the law of this state.'

Ellis sighed and shook his head, not at all happy with way things had turned out. However, he had to admit that Judge Parkes was quite in order and that there was little he could do to prevent the trial. It was not that he had any doubts as to the guilt of Amos Hutchinson and Jimmy Grover, it was simply that he believed even an obviously guilty man had the right to a proper defence. He would like to have seen a lawyer brought in to help the men prepare, but he knew that no such lawyer was available nor likely to become available.

The trial lasted precisely forty-two minutes. Ellis actually timed it. It came as no surprise when the jury did not even retire to consider their verdict, but found the two men guilty with little more than a few cursory nods.

'Amos Hutchinson and James Grover,' pronounced Judge Parkes, 'you have been found guilty of the crimes with which you have been charged. It is therefore my duty to pronounce sentence. On the charge of murder there is but one sentence I can pass, that of hanging. On the charge of theft of gold there is also only one sentence which can be handed down — hanging. I therefore sentence you to be hanged by the neck until you are dead. May God save your souls. Sentence will be carried out immediately. The court is dismissed.'

Even before the verdict had been delivered, everyone was rushing towards the door and already two ropes had been thrown over a branch of a nearby tree. Judge Parkes ordered Ellis to take the two men to the place of execution. Although he was a very unwilling participant, Ellis realized that there was absolutely nothing he could do and accompanied the two men to the tree.

'You can't let 'em kill us!' wailed Grover. 'That wasn't a fair trial. You must do something — please.'

'Unfortunately,' said Ellis, 'there is nothing I can do. The judge was quite right and the trial did conform to the legal requirements of the law. I must admit that I do not necessarily agree with the speed in which it was conducted, but Mr Parkes is the legally appointed judge in these parts and as such has every right to perform the trial providing it conforms to the law, which it does.'

'It's nothin' more'n a lynchin',' shouted Hutchinson at the gathered crowd. 'You're all murderers.'

The response of most of the other prospectors was that they, Hutchinson and Grover, were lucky to have been allowed a trial at all. They were also reminded that in other places they would have been hanged without any ceremony. The crowd plainly wanted a victim and they had got one or, in this case, two.

Two horses were brought forward and the two condemned men forced on to the bare backs, their hands tied behind them. Nooses were placed around the men's necks by two eager volunteers and the other end of the ropes tied to the bole of the tree. Despite the pleas and cries of Hutchinson and Grover, when they were ready, the two men who had appointed themselves executioners stood behind the horses and waited for a signal from Judge Parkes.

Judge Parkes once again asked God to save their souls, raised his hand and then whipped it down to his side. The two executioners slapped the rumps of the horses and shouted loudly. The horses bolted and the condemned men were suddenly dragged from the horses and swung on the ropes.

Ellis had seen hangings before, but the pure barbarity of this particular execution made him feel sick, although he did manage to control the contents of his stomach.

He heard a distinct crack as at least one neck broke under the strain. He had temporarily closed his eyes and when he looked again he saw that Jimmy Grover's body was hanging lifelessly although still swaying. Amos Hutchinson, it seemed, had not been quite so fortunate and was plainly still alive.

His legs flailed in the air and his face became reddened and apparently swelled up. One of the self-appointed executioners suddenly grabbed at Hutchinson's legs and he swung his full weight on the victim. A trickle of blood oozed from Hutchinson's mouth, his eyes stared wildly for a brief moment and then he went limp as the man released his hold on his legs. Amos Hutchinson too was now dead.

'Good God!' muttered Ellis to Apache Joe who had been at his side. 'I hope I never have to witness such a thing again.'

'You have doubts about their guilt?' asked Joe.

'No, I reckon they were guilty right enough,' said Ellis. 'It's just that it was more like a lynching than a proper hanging.'

'And that's all it was, really,' said Joe. 'A legal lynching. You were warned what would happen.'

'I know I was,' admitted Ellis. 'It's just that somehow I thought . . . well somehow I thought it would be different. I've seen hangings before — proper hangings that is — carried out by a trained hangman. This wasn't like that, it was just . . . well all I can say is it was barbaric.'

'That is the way things are away from the big city,' said Joe. 'I have seen such a thing before, when I was a boy. The man they hanged then was my father. They found him guilty of stealing a cow. He stole it because we were starving but it made no difference.'

Judge Parkes came over, smiling broadly. 'Well, they got their hanging,' he said. 'That should keep them quiet for a while.'

'Is that all it means to you,' asked Ellis, 'keeping them quiet?'

'It also means that two murderers have met their proper and just end,' said the judge. 'Anyway, you should be pleased, you can now concentrate on finding Mitchel Saunders and his men. There is, of course, still the matter of Josh Wellings.'

'You can forget all about him,' said Ellis. 'I'm taking him with me. There is just one other matter. The gold we found on Hutchinson and Grover, I'm also taking that back with me.'

'That gold is now the property of the court,' said Parkes.

'Exactly,' said Ellis. 'As the property of the court it is also the property of the state. I shall take it with me and hand it to the appropriate authorities. Don't try to blind me with any legal talk either. It goes with me and that's the end of it.'

'Very well,' said Parkes with a resigned sigh. 'If your mind is made up there is nothing I can do to stop you short of killing you myself I suppose. There is one other possibility you might care to consider.'

'I'm listening,' said Ellis.

'We split the gold between us,' said the judge. He glanced at Apache Joe and smiled. 'Three ways, of course.'

'I hear what you say, Judge,' said Ellis. 'I wonder what they will say to that suggestion back in Phoenix?'

'They don't need to know anything,' said Parkes. 'Only the three of us know exactly how much gold there is. Those men were hanged for murder, that's all that needs to be recorded.'

'My report will also say that they stole the gold,' said Ellis. 'It might also say that you, a judge, suggested dividing it.'

'Hell, Stack,' grated Parkes. 'There's enough gold there for all three of us to retire on. Don't you want that? Do you want to spend the rest of your life hunting down criminals and outlaws and possibly ending up on the wrong end of a bullet yourself? I know I don't.'

'I like my job, Mr Parkes,' replied Ellis. 'Now, hand over that gold and I'll be on my way. As you say, I do have a few outlaws to catch. Joe, you fetch Wellings and don't let anyone take him off you. You're still a deputy marshal, remember.'

Vince Parkes grudgingly handed over all the leather pouches which Ellis stowed away in his saddle-bags. Joe returned with Josh Wellings and there were a few calls for another hanging, but Ellis made it quite plain that the outlaw was going with him.

'What will you do now?' Ellis asked Joe.

'I do not think I will be safe here,' said Joe. 'It will not be long before they find an excuse to hang me as well. I have been thinking and I think that you are going to need help in finding and arresting Mitchel Saunders and his men.'

'It's not your business,' said Ellis. 'I can't ask you to risk your life any further.'

'My life is mine to risk,' said Joe. 'Besides, you have admitted yourself that you are no good at tracking. You are going to need someone like me.'

'OK, Joe,' said Ellis with a broad smile. 'Glad to have you along. Remember, you are still a deputy marshal.'

'I do not think a bullet will be able to tell the difference,' said Joe. 'We will ride out past my claim, I have a couple of things to collect.'

Josh Wellings' horse was close by and still saddled, although Ellis did note that the rifle which had been in the saddle holster was missing. He decided that it was not worthwhile trying to find out who had stolen it.

Josh Wellings was obviously relieved that he was not going to be hanged too and eagerly mounted his horse.

As they rode past the hanging tree, several of the prospectors were taking the bodies of Hutchinson and Grover down and three or four others were already digging graves close by. They stopped work for a moment and one of them made a comment about there being enough room in the graves they were digging to accommodate two more men — Wellings and Apache Joe. All three ignored the remarks and rode up to Apache Joe's claim.

'I ain't never been so shit scared in my life,' said Wellings. 'When I saw that they'd hanged those two, I thought that was what was goin' to happen to me.'

'It still might happen to you,' said Ellis. 'But at least you'll get a proper trial.'

Apache Joe collected what few belongings he possessed and then they crossed the marsh and headed north. They did not see several pairs of eyes watching their departure.

★ ★ ★

'It's them outlaws!' called one of the men digging the graves. 'They're comin' into town. Let's get the hell out of it.'

Near panic set in and all the prospectors suddenly disappeared. Mitchel Saunders and his four remaining men simply laughed at the sudden flight and pulled up outside the saloon. They burst in causing the bar girls to scream and race for their rooms. With little alternative, Vince Parkes remained behind the bar, sweating profusely.

'Hi there, gentlemen,' croaked Parkes. 'What can I get you? On the house of course.'

'Of course,' sneered Mitchel Saunders. 'Whiskies, your best, none of that moonshine rubbish.'

'Only the best Scotch,' Parkes croaked again. He poured out five good measures. 'What brings you into Mud City?'

'I guess you could call it business,' snarled Seamus Docherty, grabbing the bottle of Scotch. 'I'll take charge of that.'

'Yes, sir,' said Parkes. 'There's another couple of bottles if you want them.'

'We'll take 'em,' said Saunders. Vince Parkes reached under the counter and placed two more bottles on it. 'We just seen three men ride out of here,' continued Saunders. 'One of 'em was friend of ours, Josh Wellings. Where they goin'?'

'An' it looks like you just had yourselves a necktie party,' said Docherty, with a grin which revealed several gaps and blackened teeth. 'Sorry we missed it, I like a good hangin'. I hope they didn't die too quick. Most of the fun is seein' a man struggle on the end of a rope.'

'Yes, sir,' said Parkes. 'Allow me to introduce myself. Vince Parkes, I'm the judge around here.'

'A judge in a shit-hole like this!' exclaimed Docherty. 'So you had yourself a trial an' hanged a couple of men. What they do?'

'Murdered five prospectors and stole their gold,' croaked Parkes. 'They tried to blame it on a bunch of outlaws we think are in the area.'

'Outlaws?' said Saunders. 'We ain't seen no outlaws.' He turned to his men and laughed. 'Any of you seen any outlaws?' The men all laughed and shook their heads. 'We ain't seen no outlaws,' Saunders said to Vince Parkes.

'The man leading them is supposed to be Mitchel Saunders,' said Parkes.

'Hell now, would you believe that,' laughed Saunders, pouring himself another drink. 'Mitchel Saunders. That's one hell of a coincidence ain't it? My name's Mitchel Saunders too. Are you tryin' to say that I'm an outlaw?'

'No, sir,' whispered Parkes, now sweating even more. 'I'm sure there must be some mistake.'

'No sir!' sneered Saunders. 'Now answer my first question. Who was that ridin' out with that friend of ours?'

'That was United States Marshal Ellis Stack,' croaked Parkes. 'He reckoned that your friend — Josh Wellings — was one of the outlaws. He's gone looking for you. Er . . . I mean he's gone looking for the outlaws. The other man is an Indian called Apache Joe. Stack made him a deputy marshal.'

'A US marshal?' said Saunders. 'Seems to me this whole territory is crawlin' with US marshals.'

'I don't like marshals,' said Docherty. 'An' I especially don't like Indian deputy marshals.' He looked about the saloon. 'I seen some women runnin' away when we came in. I never met a judge what owned a saloon an' a cathouse before. Why did them women run away. Don't they like us?'

'They must have thought you were the outlaws,' said Parkes.

'Then you get 'em down here an' tell 'em we ain't,' ordered Docherty. 'I reckon the best way they can show they didn't mean to hurt our feelin's is for them to spread their legs for us — on the house of course.'

'Yes, sir,' whispered Parkes. 'I'll go tell them.'

'Don't bother,' said Saunders. He turned to one of his men. 'Lefty, you go get 'em down here an' don't go pickin' the best for yourself'

'A woman is a woman as far I'm

193

concerned,' said Lefty.

'Now what's this about some gold bein' stolen?' asked Saunders when Lefty Swann had disappeared upstairs. His question went temporarily unanswered as Lefty herded the women down the stairs. 'I'm waitin' for an answer, Judge,' said Saunders.

Vince Parkes choked slightly and wiped a cloth across his forehead. 'The men we just hanged murdered five prospectors out at a place called McFee's Basin. Like I said, they tried to blame it on . . . on these outlaws, but Marshal Stack proved it couldn't've been them, although he says they had been there and must've seen the bodies. The men we just hanged took all the gold.'

'I guess that explains a thing or two,' said Saunders. 'Where's the gold now an' how much was there?'

'Marshal Stack took it,' said Parkes. 'There was something over twenty thousand dollars' worth.'

'Twenty thou . . . ' hissed Saunders.

'That's one hell of a lot of gold an' it should've been ours. I figured somethin' like that had happened when we found them miners dead.'

'Yes, sir,' gulped Parkes. 'He's taking it back to Phoenix.'

'You mean he's goin' to hand it over, just like that? That much gold! Did you believe him?'

'Yes, sir,' Parkes said. 'I reckon Ellis Stack is just about the only man I ever met who would. I don't think there's a more honest man alive.'

Mitchel Saunders turned to his men. 'Better take them women while you can, we got us a bit of marshal-huntin' to do.'

The men needed no second telling and threw themselves at the cowering women. Mitchel Saunders did not join in but spent his time at the bar drinking and brooding. Half an hour later, the men appeared to have satisfied their lust and rejoined Saunders.

'Did you say somethin' about marshal-huntin'?' asked Seamus Docherty. 'What about a bit of judge-huntin' too. None of us have any cause to like judges. Anyhow, this particular judge just had himself some fun so I reckon we ought to have some fun too. Have you ever seen a judge swingin' on the end of a rope?'

'Can't say as I have,' said Saunders. 'They're always the ones what make other folk dance in the air.'

'Then let's have us a hangin'!' shouted Docherty. 'Hear that, fellers? We're goin' to hang a judge.'

'No ... No ... Please!' pleaded Vince Parkes. 'I've told you all I know. Marshal Stack has the gold, lots of it. You can't hang me, I haven't done anything to hurt you. I won't say a thing to anyone. You've never even been here as far as I'm concerned.'

'You must have some gold,' snarled Docherty. 'The miners all pay you in gold, you must have lots of it. Where is it?'

'It's in ... you can have it, all of it,' wailed Parkes. 'Just don't hang me

— please! It's hidden away in my office. I'll get it for you.'

'Luke,' ordered Saunders. 'Take this snivellin' bastard to get the gold an' make sure you get it all.'

Luke Franks dragged Parkes from behind the counter and marched him to his office where the judge pulled up a loose board and handed Franks two leather pouches, one full and the other about a quarter full. Franks checked that there was no more and marched Parkes back into the saloon. He handed the pouches to Saunders.

'That's all of it,' croaked Parkes. 'Please don't hurt me.'

'Oh, I don't think it'll hurt a bit,' said Saunders with a coarse laugh. He nodded at Seamus Docherty. 'Take him out an' hang him!'

Despite his screams and pleadings, Judge Vincent Parkes was dragged from the saloon to the tree where Hutchinson and Grover had been hanged and whose bodies were still to be buried. One of the ropes was thrown over the branch, a noose placed round the judge's neck. Three of the men took hold of the rope, hauled a struggling and choking Vince Parkes into the air and, after allowing him to fall a couple of times, finally tied the rope round the bole of the tree. All except Seamus Docherty returned to the saloon. Docherty appeared fascinated by the sight of Vince Parkes struggling on the end of the rope. Eventually he too returned to the saloon.

'He's dead,' he said. 'He didn't kick about as much as I've seen some others do but he died fairly slow.' He indicated the women now cowering together. 'What about them?' he asked Saunders.

'Leave 'em,' said Saunders. 'Take all the drink you can carry an' anythin' else you fancy then let's get out of here an' after that marshal an' that gold.'

As the men struggled out of the saloon under the weight of bottles, Seamus Docherty, who was the last, turned and grinned at the women.

'Goodbye, ladies,' he said, laughing.

'Sorry we couldn't stay an' show you more of what a real man is like.'

He suddenly grabbed a burning oil-lamp from a nearby shelf and threw it against a wall. Immediately flames spread up the timbers and the women ran screaming from the saloon. In a matter of minutes the whole building was burning fiercely.

9

'We saw where you'd made camp before you went into Mud City,' Ellis said to Josh Wellings. 'How do we get there? I don't expect to be given the run-around either.'

'I came in through that gap in them hills,' replied Wellings indicating a narrow gap about half a mile away. 'I reckon it's no more'n six miles.'

'What do you think, Joe?' Ellis asked Apache Joe.

'About right I would think,' replied Joe. 'I think it is the right direction. It looks narrow, how long is it?'

'Not far,' said Wellings. 'Less'n half a mile, maybe even only about a quarter of a mile. There's no need to worry about an ambush, the sides are almost sheer an' are about two hundred feet high an' there's nowhere anybody can hide.'

'For your sake,' said Ellis, 'I hope you're right. You'll be the first to die if there is any trouble.'

'I know that,' said Wellings. 'I ain't no fool, Marshal. Anyhow, I reckon that if you didn't kill me that mad bastard Seamus Docherty would. That's the kind of thing he'd do just for the hell of it. He didn't like the idea of me, Luke Franks an' Joe Daniels joinin' Saunders back in Rochester. Joe Daniels had the best idea when he ran out.'

'I met him,' said Ellis. 'Unfortunately, I was not then in a position to arrest him, so I had to let him go.'

'Some folk have all the luck,' muttered Wellings. 'You couldn't see your way to lettin' me go as well, could you Mr Stack? I ain't nobody. Sure, I'm wanted by the law for a couple of robberies, but that's all. I ain't never killed a man in my life.'

'Then all you'll get is a few years in prison,' said Ellis.

They reached the narrow pass which was, as Wellings had said, very narrow, no more than twenty feet wide, with high, almost sheer sides. After surveying the pass for a few minutes and then studying it through his spyglass, Ellis was satisfied that there was nobody there, although he would have been very surprised if there had been. Apache Joe, without being told to or asked, took the lead. Ellis took up the rear simply to keep Wellings between them.

The pass appeared to be little more than a narrow fissure, an ancient crack in the mountain, worn and widened by weathering. Once through the pass, they came into a narrow valley with a small river running through it and Wellings told them that all they had to do was follow the river upstream. The valley floor was strewn with large rocks and boulders but even so the going was fairly easy. After a time the valley widened and the rocks and boulders became less frequent. Half an hour later Apache Joe suddenly held up his hand.

'I think the camp is not far from

here,' he said. 'I remember those trees.' He indicated a small copse about half a mile ahead.

'Is that right?' Ellis asked Wellings.

'Looks it,' said Wellings. 'I ain't never been in these parts before an' I didn't take that much notice when Saunders sent me down to Mud City. It looks right though.'

'Then you and me go forward on foot,' Ellis said to Joe. 'We leave the horses and Wellings behind those rocks. Don't go thinking your luck has changed either,' he said to Wellings. 'You'll be tied up.'

'I won't try to make a run for it,' said Wellings.

'Too damned right you won't,' said Ellis.

Wellings was securely bound and both he and the horses were hidden behind a large pile of rocks. At Joe's suggestion, Wellings was also gagged to prevent him alerting the others.

Ellis kept to the side of the river they were on while Joe crossed it and made his way up the other side. Ten minutes later they were about thirty yards away from the copse. Joe suddenly disappeared but a few minutes later he returned and called to Ellis.

'They've gone,' said Joe. 'They've been here recently but they moved on. I found their tracks down this side of the river, do we follow?'

'We follow,' said Ellis. 'Damn the man.'

They returned to their horses and untied Wellings who claimed that he had no idea as to where they might have gone. He was, in Ellis's eyes, plainly not too keen to find them.

The tracks led back towards the narrow pass, although even Joe found it very difficult actually to find signs of them through valley and the pass itself. He did check that they had not carried on down the valley but found no traces. Ellis decided that it was more than likely that they had gone through the pass. Once through, the tracks became easier to follow and it was not long before both Ellis and Joe realized that they were heading back towards Mud City.

'Maybe we should have stayed and waited for them,' said Ellis. 'Did you know they intended to go there?' he asked Wellings.

'Saunders might've said somethin' about it,' admitted Wellings. 'I didn't take that much notice. He sent me into Mud City to see if I could find out anythin' about what'd been goin' on after we found them four miners dead. We didn't even look for any gold, he said it'd be a waste of time.'

'You only tried two claims that I know to,' said Ellis. 'Were there any others?' Wellings shook his head. 'I didn't think so,' continued Ellis. 'We found another miner dead and there was no sign of any of you having been there. That was the mistake the two men who killed them made.'

'Well they sure won't be makin' no more mistakes,' said Wellings with a dry laugh. 'A man don't make no bigger mistake than gettin' himself hanged. My mistake was gettin' tied up with Saunders in the first place. I didn't want to an' Joe Daniels wasn't too sure either. It was Luke Franks who talked us into it. Anyhow, we needed to get out of Rochester pretty damned quick so we went along with it.'

Still following the tracks, which wound along the side of a mountain above Big Smokey Valley, they rounded a bend when Joe suddenly stopped and pointed.

'Fire,' he said. 'I think that they must have gone into Mud City just after we left. It looks like they have set fire to the saloon. There is nothing else in Mud City which would burn like that.'

'Hell!' muttered Ellis, taking out his spyglass and looking through it. 'It's the saloon right enough,' he finally said. 'Burned to the ground. There's plenty of folk about but they look like prospectors to me. I reckon Mitchel Saunders must've left. I don't think there'd be anyone about if he was still there. I suppose we'd better get down there an' see what we can find out. I should've realized that Saunders would make his way down to Mud City. We've just wasted a lot of time.'

'That is something you could not know,' said Joe. 'We should be able to pick up his tracks from there. Somebody will have seen which way he went.'

Their return to Mud City was met with a certain amount of deep suspicion and certainly a lot of sarcastic comment about how convenient it was that they had not been there.

'Where's Vince Parkes?' Ellis asked a group of people outside the remains of the saloon.

Some of the girls and a couple of prospectors were searching about in the charred timbers. One of the prospectors suddenly laughed and held up his prize of a bottle of what appeared to be whiskey.

'Over there,' replied one of the bar girls, pointing in the direction of the hanging tree. 'They hanged him.'

'Hanged him!' exclaimed Ellis. 'Didn't anybody try to stop them?'

'Mr Stack,' sneered the girl, 'everybody was too interested in stayin' alive themselves to bother what happened to anybody else. Nobody helped Vince 'cos they knew they might get the same sort of treatment. Those men rode in just after you'd gone an' helped themselves to drink an' us girls. Then they took Vince's gold, took him outside an' strung him up. The one called Docherty seemed to really enjoy watchin' Vince struggle on the rope. I think he got more of a kick out of it than havin' sex. It was him who set fire to the place. Everythin' we owned was in there, they didn't even give us chance to save a couple of dresses. All we've got is what we stand up in an' it sure ain't much use for keepin' out the cold or wet. What the hell brings you back here anyhow?'

'We followed their tracks,' said Ellis. 'You girls must have had some gold. Did they take that too?'

'Fortunately, they didn't,' she said. 'As you can see, a couple of the girls are already searchin' through what's left in the hope they can find it.' She looked at the charred remains and sighed. 'It ain't goin' to be easy, there's no way of tellin' which was upstairs an' which was downstairs but it's there somewhere. There is just one thing, Mr Stack,' she continued, 'I heard the one they called Mitch tell the others that they were goin' on what he called marshal-huntin'. Vince had told them that you had all that gold.'

Apache Joe had wandered over to the hanging tree and called Ellis. He pointed at the strangulated, bloated features of the judge. Somebody had cut him down. 'It doesn't look as though anybody is going to bother to bury the bodies,' he said. 'From what I hear most folk are thinking about clearing out. They have this idea that Mud City is cursed. Miners are prone to such beliefs.'

'They have already dug a couple of

graves,' said Ellis. 'I think there's enough room to take Vince Parkes as well.' He called Josh Wellings over. 'Come on, you can help us dump these bodies in the graves, then you can make yourself useful and fill them in.'

When the bodies had been buried there seemed little point in hanging about. Apache Joe went ahead and eventually found the tracks left by the outlaws.

'They're heading north,' said Joe. 'Here we go again, round in circles.'

'I don't think we need bother looking for them,' said Ellis. 'One of the girls told me that Saunders was going hunting and that we are the hunted. They want this gold so I reckon it'll only be a matter of time before he finds us.'

'And you is just goin' to let him?' cried Wellings. 'Marshal, you must be almost as mad as Seamus Docherty.'

'Have you any better ideas?' asked Ellis.

'Sure,' said Wellings. 'He's headed

north so why the hell don't we head south? I think the best idea is to put as much distance between them an' us as possible. That way we might stay alive.'

'I have no intention of running away from him,' said Ellis. 'I was sent out here to do a job and I intend to do it.' He pulled alongside Apache Joe. 'You can still quit if you want to,' he said. 'I wouldn't blame you at all. After all, this isn't your responsibility and you've already been a great help.'

Apache Joe gave a dry laugh and smiled broadly. 'Mr Stack,' he said. 'You made me a deputy marshal and I've grown to like the idea. The only other time I felt useful in my life was when I was a scout with the army. No, sir, I stay with you. Besides, there's Wellings to think about. You can't look after him and take on Saunders at the same time. Not only that, but I think you might need an extra gun and I am a pretty good shot.'

'OK, Joe,' said Ellis. 'I can't say that I'm not glad to have you along. As for the idea that we head south, I think we can forget it. The quicker Saunders finds us the better. From now on keep your eyes peeled for any sign of them.'

'So you find them or they find you,' grumbled Wellings. 'There's five of them an' only two of you. You wouldn't stand a chance.'

'I'll worry about that later,' said Ellis. 'He does have a point though, Joe. Are you sure you want to stay?'

'Two guns are better than one,' replied Joe. 'I'm with you.'

They rode for the remainder of that day still following what Joe claimed were the tracks of the outlaws. Had he been on his own Ellis would not have been able to read the signs, particularly since they frequently became mingled with tracks made by those prospectors who were also heading north. However, it seemed that Joe could easily tell the difference between mule tracks and those made by horses and very few of the prospectors possessed a horse.

They eventually made camp for the

night under a small overhang of rock on the edge of a dried-up river bed which gave them a good view of the valley. There was no water to be seen but once again Apache Joe proved his worth when he cut several pieces of cactus, some of which he squeezed and then gave the resultant liquid to their horses. He gave Ellis and Wellings a large piece each and showed them how to chew on it to release the liquid. Ellis had to admit that he had tasted better but at least it did quench his thirst. Wellings stated that he had never tasted anything so disgusting but he too chewed and admitted that he felt better for it.

Joe cut some more cactus for the horses, cut off the sharp spines and left the pieces for the horses to eat. Before they settled for the night, as a precaution, Wellings was tied up.

They were on their way as soon as the first rays of sunlight streaked across the valley floor. After about an hour, Joe indicated that the horse tracks turned away from the main trail. Even Ellis could make out the tracks on this occasion and noted that they headed north-east.

'I think that one of them must know the territory,' said Joe. 'The main trail heads towards the Reese River but the way they have gone will bring them to a place known to the white man as Indian Smoke Hill. It is an old sacred place but unfortunately there are none of the old people left.'

'I know it,' said Ellis. 'That's where I met Joe Daniels. It makes some sort of sense, I suppose; it's the shortest way to Eureka. I think it's Saunders who knows the territory and he probably knows that's the way we'll have to go. If I remember right there's plenty of places they can ambush us if that's what they intend to do.'

'You mean you is prepared to walk straight into an ambush?' muttered Wellings.

'We just have to hope that Saunders doesn't realize that we are aware of it,' said Ellis. 'An ambush is only effective if somebody doesn't know.'

'You're crazy!' muttered Wellings. 'I thought you said somethin' about lettin' him find us?'

'That's what he has to think he's doing,' said Ellis.

'I only hope you two know what you is doin' as well,' muttered Wellings. 'I'll be honest, I don't reckon my chances are too good with Saunders. If he does get his hands on that gold you're carryin' he won't want too many people around to share it with. I reckon him an' Docherty will kill the others an' keep the gold themselves. Who knows, it could even be that one of 'em will end up killin' the other. I just don't want to be there when it happens no matter how much gold there is.'

It was approaching sunset when they saw Indian Smoke Hill which, Ellis well knew from recent experience, was further away than it appeared. He ordered camp to be made for the night alongside a small pool of water.

Josh Wellings complained of feeling

hungry and once again it was Apache Joe who came to the rescue. He disappeared for a few minutes and when he returned he was carrying two dead rattlesnakes.

'They make very good eating,' he said. 'It does mean lighting a fire though.'

'You expect me to eat snake?' said Wellings, with a grimace.

'I do not expect you eat anything you do not want to, my friend,' replied Joe. 'If you are hungry you will eat. It does not matter to me what you do. I have no interest in keeping you alive.'

'OK, Joe,' said Ellis. 'I've eaten rattler enough times before. It isn't my favourite but at least it's food. We'll light a fire. I don't fancy raw rattler. Wellings, go see if you can find some wood. There's plenty of brush about and I think I saw some wood a few yards back.'

'They'll see it from miles away,' complained Wellings.

'Good,' said Ellis. 'I was beginning to

wonder if that girl had been right about them hunting us. This way it will make them think that we don't know and will tell them where we are if they see the flames or smoke. Now do as you're told and find some brush and wood. Don't even think about trying to make a run for it either. I can assure you we'd catch you before you'd even gone a hundred yards.'

Despite the horrified look on Wellings's face when handed a piece of cooked rattlesnake, he soon changed his ideas and admitted that it really tasted quite good. The water from the pool was tepid but nevertheless most welcome. In the absence of any grass or shoots for the horses to eat, Joe once again cut some pieces of cactus for them.

'I never thought about feeding horses that way,' said Ellis. 'I must remember it. They seem to like it.'

'Just remember to cut off the spines,' said Joe. 'It is an old Indian way. The snake too. There is food and water even in the driest desert if you know where to look. Snake is the best but there are lizards too. There is not much meat on a lizard but at least it is something to eat.'

'I heard of a tribe who carry bags of insects and bugs around with them,' said Ellis. 'I hear they actually eat things like that.'

'There is such a tribe,' said Joe. 'That kind of food is not something that my people would eat, but if that is all there is to eat, then it must be eaten.'

The night passed without incident and they were on their way as soon as dawn broke. Ellis had been right about Indian Smoke Hill being further away than it appeared and it took them almost three hours before they were within a mile of it. Ellis called a halt and examined the hill through his spyglass.

'No sign of them as far as I can see,' he said. 'Take a look, Joe, maybe you can see something I couldn't.'

Apache Joe scanned the area and

announced that as far as he could tell, there was nobody about. Even so, Ellis ordered that they proceed slowly and with caution. They reached the base of the hill, still following the tracks of the outlaws and, after a brief search by Apache Joe, he announced that they had moved on.

'They made camp here for the night,' he said. 'The embers of their fire are still warm. They cannot be too far ahead.'

'Which means they could be anywhere up ahead,' muttered Wellings. 'It looks like good ambush country to me.'

'It is,' said Ellis. 'I came this way before. What do you think, Joe?' he asked Apache Joe.

'I think that our friend is right,' said Joe. 'I too know this country and there are many places where they could hide.'

'Then what do you suggest?' asked Ellis.

'If you want them to find us then we keep on riding straight ahead,' said Joe. 'And the alternative?' asked Ellis.

'I know a way round,' said Joe. 'The ground is more open about ten miles ahead which should give us the advantage.'

'And it's still a long way to Eureka,' said Ellis. 'I think we ought to go round. I know I said I wanted them to find us but I'd rather they found us somewhere where we would stand a better chance.'

'That's the first sensible thing I've heard you say,' grunted Wellings. 'Better still, I say we ride like hell for this Eureka place.'

'You seem very eager to get to prison,' said Ellis.

'Stayin' alive in prison is better'n bein' dead out here,' grumbled Wellings. 'Not much better but it wouldn't be for ever like bein' dead would be.'

'OK, we go round,' said Ellis. 'If we manage to get in front of them it will give us the advantage. Lead on, Joe.'

For another half-hour, Apache Joe led them south before turning up along a dry river-bed which took them in a more easterly direction. Eventually the river-bed disppeared and they found themselves on a high, windy plain. There was little chance of anyone being able to ambush them.

It took them the remainder of the day to cross the plain and they eventually found a clear pool of water where Ellis decided to make camp for the night. Apache Joe looked for something to eat but on this occasion he was unable to find anything. He made some wry comment about there being plenty of grubs and insects if they were hungry enough to eat them. Both Ellis and Wellings declined.

The following morning took them through some low hills and, although ambush was always possible, Ellis did not think it likely, especially as Joe had not found any signs that anyone had been that way. Once through the hills they descended into a wide valley which Ellis thought he recognized.

'The question is, are we ahead of them or behind them?' said Ellis. 'I'm relying on you to find their tracks, Joe.'

Joe had already been examining the ground but had so far found nothing. He rode on ahead but half an hour later declared that there were no tracks.

'That does not mean that they have not been here,' he explained. 'The valley is wide and there could easily be tracks. It would take too long to search the whole valley.'

'Then I suggest that we carry on towards Eureka,' said Ellis. 'I have this feeling that they aren't too far away, though. Keep your eyes and ears open. You too, Wellings.'

Half an hour later, Joe suddenly held up his hand and stopped. He rode to the top of a small ridge and looked back. After a time he rejoined the other two.

'I think they are behind us,' he said. 'The signs are that several horses come this way and they do not travel slowly.'

'That could mean they caught sight of us somehow,' said Ellis. 'What alerted you, Joe?'

'Nothing more than a feeling in my bones,' replied Joe. 'It is hard to explain, but it is something which most Indians possess.' He looked about. 'There is nowhere to hide. We must ride fast.'

'No!' said Ellis, firmly. 'As you say, this is open country. They wouldn't risk getting too close even though there are only two of us.'

'Three!' said Wellings.

'Only two of us with guns,' Ellis pointed out.

'Then give me a gun,' said Wellings. 'I ain't too bad a shot.'

'And risk you shooting us?' said Ellis. 'You must think I'm crazy.'

'Haven't I been sayin' you're crazy all along?' said Wellings. 'Don't worry about me killin' you. If you want Saunders I reckon you're goin' to need all the help you can get.'

'He is right,' said Joe. 'We have two rifles and two pistols each. He can have his own pistol although it will not be much use unless they come very close.

He can be placed between us, that way if he tries to shoot one of us the other can shoot him. You must make up your mind, Marshal. They will be upon us very soon.'

'OK,' sighed Ellis. 'I guess even a man like him has to be trusted sometime.' He took Wellings's gun from his saddle-bag and handed it to him. He also gave him a box of bullets. 'Just remember, at the first hint of you getting ideas about killing either of us, you'll be the one who ends up dead.'

'Marshal,' said Wellings, 'I reckon I'm goin' to end up dead if Saunders gets his hands on me. Before I go though I really would like to take that bastard Seamus Docherty with me.'

10

It was about ten minutes before Mitch Saunders and his men appeared over the crest of a small rise. On seeing the three men in front of them, Mitch Saunders called his men to a halt about fifty yards away. For several minutes the opposing groups faced each other in silence.

'You almost had us fooled,' Mitch Saunders suddenly called out. 'We saw you out at Indian Smoke Hill but when you didn't show up along the main trail I guessed what had happened. You might as well give up now, Marshal. You don't stand a chance.'

'And what sort of chance do we stand if we do surrender?' called Ellis. 'I'll tell you — none. You have a lot of murders on your hands, Saunders, including the murders of a US marshal and five of his deputies and a legally appointed judge. Killing another marshal and his deputy won't make any difference to what will happen to you.'

'Too true,' called Saunders with a coarse laugh. 'Anyhow, why only five deputies? I counted six plus that fool Tom Burns.'

'One of them survived,' replied Ellis. 'His testimony will be enough to see you on the end of a rope.'

'I could've sworn they were all dead,' said Saunders. 'Still, it don't matter none to you, you won't be around to see what happens. Just one thing, Marshal, we didn't have nothin' to do with them miners bein' killed.'

'I know that, we caught the men who did it,' replied Ellis. 'You must have seen their bodies back at Mud City.'

'We saw 'em,' admitted Saunders. 'Just settin' the record straight, that's all. Now, you can do this the easy way or the hard way. You hand over that gold you're carryin' an' I promise you we'll kill you quick an' clean. Either way you is goin' to die so you might as well go quick.'

'If we are going to die, Saunders,' said Ellis, 'I'll make sure that as many of you as possible come with us, starting with you.' Ellis then called to the men with Saunders. 'Don't think that he is going to give a damn about which of you gets killed. All he's interested in is the gold and keeping it all for himself. The more of you who die means a bigger share for those left alive and I think he'll make sure that he is the only one left. He doesn't intend to share the gold with any of you, including you, Docherty.'

'Nice try, Marshal,' called Saunders with another coarse laugh. 'You'll never know if that's true or not.'

'He's right,' Josh Wellings suddenly called out. 'You'll be the first, Luke. Neither him nor Docherty liked the idea of you, me an' Joe Daniels joinin' him in Rochester.'

'So, we have a turncoat,' said Saunders. 'Hear that, fellers? Josh has thrown his lot in with the law. It looks like they've even trusted you with a gun as well. No matter, five against three are the kind of odds I'll take any time.'

Quite suddenly, Lefty Swann pointed behind Ellis, Joe and Wellings. Mitch Saunders swore loudly and fired at Ellis. The bullet missed but Saunders was suddenly ordering his men to 'Get the hell out of it!' At the same time Ellis became aware of the thunder of many horses.

Another volley of shots followed Saunders's order and Josh Wellings fell to the ground clutching at his shoulder. Three of the outlaws were already fleeing before Saunders and Docherty had even turned their horses. Both Ellis and Joe fired after the fleeing men but did not know if they had hit any of them. Ellis turned to see a troop of soldiers bearing down on them.

'The army!' exclaimed Ellis. 'What the hell brings them out here?'

'Whatever it is, I am most grateful,' said Apache Joe.

A few minutes later a troop of cavalry

thundered up. At first they carried on past the three men and in pursuit of the outlaws but a short time later they returned.

'Unfortunately it appears that we have lost them among all the rocks and boulders. They could be anywhere and I am not prepared to risk the lives of my men,' panted the young officer who was in command. 'Marshal Ellis Stack?' he asked. Ellis nodded. 'Lieutenant Quincy, Twenty-Fourth US Cavalry out of Eureka. It looks like we arrived just in time.'

'It would certainly seem so,' said Ellis. 'How did you know I was here?'

'We didn't,' replied Lieutenant Quincy. 'We were on a routine patrol when my sergeant spotted what was going on. I only guessed it was you. I had been told to keep an eye open for you. All patrols out this way had been told the same. It seems that you have friends in powerful places.'

'General Ives?' asked Ellis.

'That's where the order came from, I

believe,' said Quincy. 'Were those men the escaped prisoners?'

'They were,' said Ellis. 'I thought the army weren't going to get involved in what they said was a civil matter.'

'I wouldn't know anything about that, Marshal,' replied the lieutenant. 'I know standing orders are not to become involved in civil matters though. All I was told was to keep an eye open for you and provide assistance if needed.'

'Then you can assist by helping me catch those men,' said Ellis.

'Sorry, Marshal,' said the lieutenant. 'I know I'd be overstepping my authority if I did that. My orders are to keep out of any civil matters. I'll willingly escort you back to Eureka, but that's all.'

'But they murdered US Marshal Tom Burns and five of his deputies and then they murdered a judge. Those kinds of murders are outside what the army call civil matters and they can act.'

'You might be right,' admitted Quincy. 'The only trouble is I would need the direct authority of my commanding officer and I do know that we know nothing about any such killings. If I take my men out there I'll be putting their lives at risk and I could end up on a charge of neglect of duty.'

'You can take my word for it,' said Ellis. 'I'll take full responsibility.'

'Sorry, Mr Stack,' said Quincy. 'I still need the authority of a senior officer. Now, it's a long way back to Eureka. Let's go.'

'No,' said Ellis. 'I'm going after those outlaws. That's what I was sent out here to do. Finding and arresting those men is *my* duty, that's what marshals do and, like you, I obey orders.'

'That's up to you,' said Quincy with a shrug. 'Just don't expect the army to be on hand the next time you find yourself in trouble, that's all.'

'I won't,' said Ellis with a resigned sigh. 'I'm not going back with you, but you can take Apache Joe and Wellings.' By that time Wellings had struggled to his feet and did not appear to be too badly hurt. 'Wellings is under arrest as a member of the gang who murdered Marshal Tom Burns — '

'I already told you!' wailed Wellings. 'I didn't kill any of 'em.'

'That's for the judge to decide,' said Ellis. 'There is one more thing you can do, Lieutenant,' Ellis continued. 'I have some bags of gold, a hell of a lot of gold. I want you to take it to Eureka and hand it over for safe-keeping. That's what Saunders and his men were after.'

'Gold! OK, Marshal,' agreed Quincy. 'I guess I can do that. I'll hand Wellings over to the sheriff. The gold had better be kept at the fort. What about the Indian?'

'The Indian goes with Marshal Stack,' replied Joe.

The lieutenant looked surprised, as if it was something unusual for an Indian to answer for himself. 'Is that right, Marshal?' he asked.

'If that's what he says, then that's OK with me,' replied Ellis. 'Joe is a deputy marshal.'

'I've never heard of an Indian deputy marshal before,' said Quincy. 'If that's what you want though, who am I to argue?'

'Who indeed?' replied Ellis.

He handed the bags of gold to the lieutenant who made a comment about there being enough to tempt any man but that he would ensure it and Josh Wellings would be delivered. He then ordered his men back to Eureka.

Ellis and Joe waited until the patrol was out of sight before talking about their next move. It was finally decided to give Mitch Saunders time to get well clear before following.

'We want them to think we went with the patrol,' said Ellis. 'You should be able to follow their trail. Which way do you think they'll go?'

'If Saunders knows the territory,' said Joe. 'I think he'll head for a place called Badwater. There's nothing there except what used to be a staging-post. It isn't used by the stage company now but the man who owns it still lives there. He makes a living by trapping for furs and selling food and drink to the occasional traveller. A word of warning, Mr Stack. If we do get that far, don't eat or drink anything he might offer. You are more likely to die of poisoning than a bullet. He also has a wife and daughter. Both are available to any passing stranger — at a price — but personally I'd be afraid of catching something unpleasant.'

'Why should Saunders go there?' asked Ellis.

'Because there is nowhere else to go,' said Joe. 'He will go there to make plans. You said that it is thought he intends to kill the governor. I think that he now needs to consider his position again and Badwater is the ideal place for a man like him to think. Heinrich Klebber — he's a German I believe — is not particular about the company he keeps.'

'How far?' asked Ellis.

'We should get there by noon tomorrow,' replied Joe.

Joe soon picked up the tracks left by the fleeing outlaws and seemed satisfied that they were indeed heading for Badwater. That night they made camp alongside a small, clear pool and Joe quickly located two large rattlesnakes for food.

About two hours after starting off the following morning, they found the remains of a fire and Joe was quite certain that it had been made by the outlaws.

'We are no more than two hours behind them,' said Joe. 'Since they made no attempt to hide the fire, I believe they are not expecting anybody to follow them.'

'There's plenty of places they can hide,' said Ellis. 'From now on we take it slow and keep an eye open for them.'

Joe stooped down and examined the ground, dabbing his finger into something. He looked up and smiled. 'One of them is injured,' he said. 'I think he bleeds quite badly.'

'Good,' said Ellis. 'He'll be less trouble.'

Half an hour later they discovered that the injured man would certainly be no problem to them at all. They came upon his body lying next to a thorntree and already it was the subject of much interest to several buzzards and countless flies. As well as a wound in his upper back, it was plain that he had been murdered. There was a large wound in the back of his head.

'Saunders didn't want a cripple with him,' observed Ellis. 'A bullet in his head saw to that.'

'Do you recognize him?' asked Joe.

'I think it must be the one called Luke Franks,' said Ellis, taking the pictures of the four escaped prisoners from his pocket and comparing the likenesses. 'Yes, I'm sure of it. His is the only picture I don't have.'

'What do we do with him?' asked Joe. 'They've taken his horse and his guns.'

'What can we do with him?' asked Ellis. 'We can't take him with us. I suppose we ought to bury him.'

'Why bother?' said Joe. 'The buzzards will soon dig him up again and it will not be long before the coyotes catch his scent which means that it will not be long before all that will remain will be a few bones.'

'I guess you're right,' said Ellis. 'OK, we leave him.' He looked at the buzzards standing patiently nearby. 'It's breakfast-time!' he called to them. 'OK, Joe, so now there are only four of them. The odds are getting better all the time.'

They did not travel fast, Ellis possibly being overcautious in suspecting an ambush almost anywhere. The result was that they did not reach Badwater until about three o'clock in the afternoon.

When they did arrive at a ridge which overlooked the solitary, ramshackle but surprisingly large building alongside a small lake, they kept well out of sight. Ellis surveyed the building with his spyglass.

It appeared that the four remaining outlaws were in the building but there was no other sign of them. The paddock behind the building contained six horses, five of which Ellis assumed belonged to the outlaws. There were also five saddles hanging over the paddock fence.

'They must be in there,' said Ellis, handing the spyglass to Joe. 'We have to flush them out somehow or keep them holed up in there and pick them off one at a time.'

'Or wait for them to come out,' said Joe. 'It's two against four and you tell me that Seamus Docherty is very good and very accurate with a gun. It would be better to get them into the open. It is quite a large building; I have been inside and I know there are many places a man can hide.'

'I'm ready to listen to any ideas,' said Ellis. 'I'd like to take them back alive if possible but if I can't then I don't mind taking their bodies back.'

'Then we must get closer,' said Joe.

238

He pointed at the remains of a wagon almost opposite the front door of the building and about thirty yards from it. 'One of us needs to get behind that. Do you think you can get there without being seen?'

'If I circle round until it's between me and them, I ought to make it,' said Ellis. 'What will you do?'

'I will be what you white folk call the bait,' said Joe. 'Do not concern yourself about me. I will wait for half an hour to allow you to get in position.'

'I hope you know what you're doing, Joe,' said Ellis. 'Remember, this isn't really your concern.'

'I am a deputy marshal, am I not?' said Joe with a broad grin. 'Outlaws are the concern of all deputy marshals. Now go, trust me.'

Ellis looked at his deputy for a few moments and then nodded. He held out his hand which Joe took.

'Just in case things don't work out,' Ellis said. 'Thanks for everything you've done, Joe.'

'Everything will be all right,' assured Joe. 'Now go.'

Ellis dropped out of sight of the building and made his way along the ridge. Eventually he looked over and judged it safe enough to make his way down. There were quite a number of bushes about and he dashed from one to another. After some time he found himself in a direct line with the broken wagon and the door of the building. There did not appear to be any windows on that side of the building. Getting into position behind the wagon was easy enough and brought him to within thirty yards of the building. He looked up at the ridge but there was no sign of Apache Joe. He was not surprised.

Seemingly out of nowhere, Apache Joe suddenly appeared, on his horse, to Ellis's left about fifty or sixty yards from the building. Had it not been for the fact that Ellis recognized Joe, he might well have thought that another Indian had arrived. Joe had changed his clothes and was now dressed in traditional Apache garb.

Joe remained on his horse, his rifle-butt resting on his thigh, obviously hoping to attract the attention of the outlaws. He remained there for several minutes.

The door of the building suddenly opened and four men staggered out, two of them, including Mitch Saunders, clutching bottles. They swayed unsteadily for a few moments, staring at Apache Joe. Mitch Saunders took a drink from his bottle, wiped his sleeve across his mouth and staggered forward a few steps, almost falling in the process.

'What the hell do you want, you filthy Indian bastard?' called Saunders. Apache Joe remained silent. 'Don't you understand English?' demanded Saunders, swaying unsteadily. Again Joe remained silent This silence seemed to annoy Saunders and he growled something at the men with him.

By this time a man and two women had appeared at the door and seemed to be enjoying the situation, the women urging Saunders to kill Joe.

'Seems like he don't understand,' rasped Seamus Docherty, who did not appear quite as drunk as the others. 'He'll understand this though. Even a dumb Indian knows what a bullet is.'

Docherty drew his gun and fired a shot at Joe, who again remained silent and did not move. He had calculated his distance well as the bullet raised dirt about five yards short of him.

'Get the bastard an' skin him alive!' snarled Jimmy Coburn, taking a few steps forward and drawing his gun. The others followed him.

'Kill his horse!' ordered Saunders, taking aim at the animal's head.

★　★　★

There was single shot and the gun in Saunders's hand flew into the air, followed by a howl of pain. Saunders clutched at his hand and all four stared in the direction of the wagon. Apache

Joe took the opportunity to move further away. One of the women screamed and ran inside the building, quickly followed by the man and the other woman.

'You might as well give up now, Saunders,' called Ellis. 'You'll never make it back inside.'

'Stack!' yelled Saunders. 'You never give up, do you?' He called to the other three with him. 'Forget the Indian, I want Stack! You should've gone with the army, Marshal,' he called to Ellis. 'That way you would've stayed alive. This way you is nothin' but buzzard meat.'

'Just like Luke Franks,' called Ellis.

'He couldn't make it,' snarled Saunders. 'He'd taken a bullet in his back. Seamus just put him out of his misery like he would an injured horse.'

'I guessed that was the case,' said Ellis. 'The difference is I'm not injured.'

'Maybe not, but you'll soon be beggin' to be put out of your misery,' called Saunders. 'This time though there ain't nobody goin' to put a bullet in your head. I wanna watch you die real slow.'

'It's three against two now,' Ellis called again. 'I don't think you'll be able to handle a gun for quite some time.'

'I got news for you,' called Saunders. 'I can use both hands.' He suddenly bent down, picked up his gun and charged forward. 'Come on, you scum,' he shouted at his companions. 'Come on, he can't take all of us.'

Lefty Swann took a few steps forward but stopped when he saw that neither Seamus Docherty nor Jimmy Coburn had moved. Mitch Saunders was so enraged that he did not notice that he was alone. Suddenly Docherty, Swann and Coburn were running back to the building.

Jimmy Coburn was the first to fall as Apache Joe raised his rifle and fired. Lefty Swann was next to sprawl in the dirt as Joe fired again. Another shot from Joe appeared to hit Docherty, but he kept his balance and crashed through the door of the building. Both Coburn and Swann remained on the ground, apparently lifeless.

The shooting had brought Mitch Saunders to a standstill about ten yards from the wagon. He looked about despairingly for a few moments. Ellis could easily have taken him out, but he wanted to take the outlaw alive if at all possible and held his fire.

Saunders suddenly gave a somewhat hysterical laugh, pulled another bottle from his jacket-pocket, used his teeth to pull out the cork, and took a long drink, somehow holding the bottle in his injured hand.

'Cowards, all of 'em!' he laughed, plainly finding it difficult to remain on his feet. 'You can have 'em, Marshal, I was goin' to kill 'em all anyway. First though there's just the little matter of killin' you.' He took another drink and then threw the bottle to one side. 'There's plenty more inside,' he said, laughing. 'Come on, Stack, let's see just how good you are face to face. That shot of yours was nothin' more'n luck.'

'You're too drunk, Saunders,' said Ellis, standing up, his rifle in one hand and his Colt in the other. 'Give up now or I might have to kill you.'

'It's you or me, Marshal, I don't intend to let anybody hang me or send me back to prison. Do your damnedest, Stack.' He raised his gun and slowly took aim at Ellis but he did not have time to squeeze the trigger.

Ellis deliberately aimed for Saunders' shoulder, not wishing to kill him. The shot was accurate and Saunders crashed to the ground swearing loudly but still managing to keep hold of his gun. Ellis slowly moved forward, his gun at the ready, and was eventually standing over Saunders.

The outlaw laughed coarsely and somehow managed to raise his gun. Ellis had little choice but to shoot again and this time the bullet slammed into Saunders' upper chest. The outlaw gave a brief laugh before his eyes closed and the gun dropped from his hand. Ellis kicked the gun to one side and bent down to examine Saunders. He was still alive.

'What about the other two?' Ellis called to Joe.

'They don't move,' replied Joe. 'I think they are dead. I know I shot to kill.'

'I don't think Saunders is going to make it,' said Ellis. 'It was almost as though he wanted me to kill him. That just leaves Seamus Docherty.'

'He has Klebber and the women inside,' said Joe. 'From what I hear I think he will try to use them as hostages.'

Ellis walked across to Joe and for some time both of them studied the old staging-post.

'I suppose we could just sit here and wait,' said Ellis. 'He can't stay holed up in there for ever. Personally I'm not too bothered if he does try to use them as hostages. They seemed to be all in favour of killing you.'

'Klebber does not like Indians,' said Joe. 'But I don't know how he feels about killing US marshals.'

'He probably couldn't care less as long as he doesn't do the killing,' said Ellis. 'You go round the back, I don't want Docherty trying to make a break for it. I'll cover the front. If he does come out, I leave it to you to do what you think best.'

Joe circled round until he was behind the paddock and when Ellis saw that he was in position, he moved forward a few yards and called to Docherty.

'Your friends are no use to you now,' Ellis called. 'I know you are injured and you probably need a doctor. Give yourself up, Docherty.'

'Go shit, Stack!' came the reply. 'I ain't goin' back to no prison. If you want me, you come an' get me. Just remember, I've got two women here an' I ain't afraid to kill 'em if I have to.'

Although Ellis had told Joe that he was not bothered about the women being used as hostages, his instincts were that he could not allow them to be put at risk. 'Let them go,' called Ellis. 'If you do, I'll make sure it goes in your favour. It could mean the difference between hanging and a prison sentence.'

There was a laugh from inside the building followed by a scream from one of the women.

'Have you ever been in prison, Marshal?' called Docherty. 'I think I'd rather die than go back there.'

'As a matter of fact I have,' called Ellis. 'I was sentenced for something I didn't do. Fortunately it was proved I didn't do it, but not before I'd served my time. I know how you feel, Docherty, but a few years in prison is better than being dead.'

'Then you know what goes on in places like that,' called Docherty. 'I think bein' dead is better. Anyhow, why should you bother about what happens to Klebber an' his women? They sure as hell didn't give a damn what happened to you an' that Indian. Saunders even told me that Klebber uses Indians to feed to his hogs.'

Ellis looked towards the paddock but there was no sign of Apache Joe. He cursed, knowing that Joe had decided to act on his own.

★ ★ ★

Joe had taken the opportunity of slipping between a few loose boards at the back of the building while Ellis was talking to Docherty. Having been inside on other occasions, he knew the layout.

'I know Klebber feeds Indians to his pigs,' Joe called from the gloomy depths, 'One of them was my brother. Do you remember me, Klebber, Jottie Washakie? My brother was Mattie Washakie.'

'Indian names mean nothing to me,' growled Klebber. 'He's in here,' he called to Docherty.

'I can hear that, you idiot,' snapped Docherty. 'You damned well find him an' kill him if you want your women to stay alive.' He called to Ellis. 'That damned Indian friend of yours is in here, Stack. You tell him to get his ass outside. If he don't, I kill these women.'

'Joe is his own man,' replied Ellis. 'The best thing you can do is give yourself up, Docherty.'

'Go shit, Stack!' called Docherty. 'I'll see all of 'em dead first.'

In the meantime, Klebber was slowly inching his way through the gloom towards the rear of the building, carrying an oil-lamp. It was something of a labyrinth of stalls and what were once very rough sleeping quarters for stage-passengers. Dry straw and hay lay in abundance.

'Over here!' called Joe. Klebber swung round. 'Not there, here!' Joe called again. 'Over by the pens where you kept your pigs, where you cut up my brother and fed him to them.'

'Bastard!' grated Klebber. 'If I still had my pigs I would feed you to them as well. Show yourself.'

'Behind you!' said Joe.

Klebber swung round to meet Joe's fist slamming into his face. As he went down, the oil-lamp flew from his hand and landed in a pile of dry straw. In a matter of seconds flames were spreading out of control. Joe laughed and moved away.

'What the hell's goin' on?' yelled Docherty as smoke started to fill the building. 'You are going to burn alive,' said Joe. 'The choice is yours, burn or a bullet.'

'Bastard!' Docherty yelled. 'Just remember, if I burn, they burn as well.'

'Then they must burn,' replied Joe. 'Klebber killed my brother. I have waited a long time for this moment. Klebber's wife is no better than him. It was she who told him to feed the body of my brother to his pigs.'

'Don't you pay no heed to him!' screamed a woman. 'If it was his brother, it was because he tried to . . . '

A huge explosion sent wood and debris high into the air and Ellis was forced to run for cover behind the old wagon. When everything settled down he found himself running towards the remains of the still-burning building, calling for Joe.

A burning piece of timber moved and Joe's face appeared. Somehow Ellis managed to get to him and haul him out. Apart from a small burn to his upper left arm, Joe did not appear to be injured. A few more timbers moved and both men helped the two women out of the wreckage, the only signs of injury to either being a slight burn on the older woman's hand. There was no sign of Klebber or Docherty.

★   ★   ★

It was the following morning before Joe and Ellis discovered the bodies of Docherty and Klebber. Klebber had plainly perished in the fire and was totally beyond recognition. Seamus Docherty had escaped the flames but they found a fairly large piece of shattered wood embedded in his back, obviously the result of wood flying as the explosion occured. According to Mrs Klebber, there had been a large amount of dynamite stored in the building.

Mitch Saunders, Lefty Swann and Jimmy Coburn were also dead and Ellis rather felt that he had failed in that he now had only bodies to take back. A search of the bodies found the two leather pouches of gold on Saunders, one full and one about a quarter full.

'What will you do now?' Ellis asked Joe.

'I think my work is done, my friend,' said Joe. 'Here we must part. Thanks to you, my brother's death is avenged. I had thought of killing Klebber many times but I could not commit murder.'

'I guess it's the best way,' admitted Ellis. 'I couldn't have got this far if it hadn't been for you though.' He fingered the two leather pouches and smiled. 'I did promise that you would be paid for your services, Joe.' He suddenly tossed both pouches to the

Indian. 'This ought to see you right.'

'I thank you, my friend,' said Joe, 'but I do not want to get you into trouble.'

'Nobody knows about that gold except you and me,' said Ellis. 'Now, help me load the bodies on to the horses. It's a long way to Eureka and I want to get there before they get too high.'

THE END

We do hope that you have enjoyed reading this large print book.

Did you know that all of our titles are available for purchase?

We publish a wide range of high quality large print books including:
Romances, Mysteries, Classics
General Fiction
Non Fiction and Westerns

Special interest titles available in large print are:
The Little Oxford Dictionary
Music Book, Song Book
Hymn Book, Service Book

Also available from us courtesy of Oxford University Press:
Young Readers' Dictionary
(large print edition)
Young Readers' Thesaurus
(large print edition)

For further information or a free brochure, please contact us at:
Ulverscroft Large Print Books Ltd.,
The Green, Bradgate Road, Anstey,
Leicester, LE7 7FU, England.
Tel: (00 44) **0116 236 4325**
Fax: (00 44) **0116 234 0205**

A TOWN CALLED TROUBLESOME

John Dyson

Matt Matthews had carved his ranch out of the wild Wyoming frontier. But he had his troubles. The big blow of '86 was catastrophic, with dead beeves littering the plains, and the oncoming winter presaged worse. On top of this, a gang of desperadoes had moved into the Snake River valley, killing, raping and rustling. All Matt can do is to take on the killers single-handed. But will he escape the hail of lead?

GAMBLER'S BULLETS

Robert Lane

The conquering of the American west threw up men with all the virtues and vices. The men of vision, ready to work hard to build a better life, were in the majority. But there were also work-shy gamblers, robbers and killers. Amongst these ne'er-do-wells were Melvyn Revett, Trevor Younis and Wilf Murray. But two determined men — Curtis Tyson and Neville Gough — took to the trail, and not until their last bullets were spent would they give up the fight against the lawless trio.